THE HUNTED

MORETTI SIBLINGS BOOK 3

K.J. THOMAS

Editor: Samantha Wiley

Proofreader: Rachel

Cover Artist: Thomas Moore Jr.

❦ Created with Vellum

CHAPTER 1

*a*nna

Tingles start to dance over my skin, as the inside of my head knocks-like an unwanted solicitor. *Are you sure you want to do this?* I've asked myself this question multiple times in the last five minutes. If I make, even a minuscule, mistake tonight, it will mean the end of me and most likely the innocent woman I'm trying to save.

Still, I wouldn't change anything. There is no other place I would rather be than here, even though I don't realize that, I'm about to get my ass handed to me. Four men against one woman seems pretty fair, *right?*

Four tanks, well three, their leader is a pussy, a grossly-lanky man. Most people consider me thin and ladylike. My four older brothers love this. Not many people outside of our family business realize I'm a trained killer. Even though I've never killed...*yet.*

1

I'm not a mercenary, I don't go around killing warlords and your basic disgusting criminals. Our family is more for the victim's side. We intervene with hopes of no blood being shed. If there's no choice, we've all been trained for anything.

I take deep cleansing breaths with my back plastered against the wall. The lights are out in the obscene house. The place reminds me of a glorified jail for the rich built solely of cement. My cheek pressed against the coarse brick brownstone as I inch along. I can hear the frozen crunch of grass blades underneath my boots while I move. The brittle brick digs into my face as I try to remain hidden, keeping my body as one with the building.

My hand inches down my side to check for my knife that is strapped inside my right thigh. I never carry a gun; doesn't mean I don't know how to use them I just prefer my knives.

The backside of the brownstone is eerily quiet. I've been studying this place for weeks and there's always noise, either it is from the asshole men or the screams from Sophia. My eyes close thinking of her, I can only guess what she's gone through. The waiting to finally get here to help has been excruciating.

This cold and unwelcoming place is one of money, old money. I needed to borrow my brother, Jax's, Bentley just-so I would fit in during stakeouts. Me driving around here in an older model Jeep wasn't going to cut it. Being in the Bentley I felt like the biggest idiot in the world. Who really wants to drive this ostentatious thing?

We tried to get cameras inside, but Mr. Prick is far too cautious to let anybody in his home. Nothing worked from deliveries to electricians-even an old lady needing help. He refused to open the door.

It almost feels like nobody's home, but I'm not taking any chances. I reach into my backpack and grab my tools-so I can break in. I would prefer just to smash the window, but noise and all.

I'm currently dressed in all black from my cargo pants to my black combat boots. I'm wearing a very tight black Henley sweatshirt. It's October here in New York and there's a bite of chill in the air.

The only thing that gives off any color is my pale skin and the bright green of my eyes, which are currently closed.

The deep breathing exercises are what my father taught us how to do-to relax, basically get our heads where they need to be-rescue and survivor mode. One last final deep breath, it's time to get to work. I text my brother Jax.

Me: BAB going in.

BAB is short for badass bitch. We were supposed to come up with our own code names and I couldn't think of anything else. My brothers laughed, they thought it was hilarious. Most of the other ops don't know what it stands for.

The door pushes open with a creek, making me

wince. The reticent of this place is messing with my head. Noise would be greatly appreciated at least I would know what I'm walking into or where I'm heading. Silence can be deadly, usually only meaning one of two things: nobody's around or they're waiting for you.

The brownstone's been fixed up and modernized, everything is now cement white, gray or black, including the countertops. I creep along, making my way to the boring, cold kitchen.

I've spent time studying the blueprints of this place. Even when you update or modernize, the new blueprints have to be turned into the city, which is mostly for public viewing depending on who you are. If not, we have people that can get a hold of the new ones for us.

I've been getting myself into the same headspace as the kidnapping rapist. I would want somebody where it's quieter and easier to clean up any wanted or unwanted messes. I'd put the person in the basement. Unless I'm a sadistic creep and not just obsessed with one woman, I'd build soundproof rooms.

From our research, Jared has been watching Sophia for a few years. That doesn't leave much time to attack and kidnap other women.

I move my hand up to my throat feeling my heartbeat. Not surprisingly it's moving much faster. An eerie sensation is making the hair on my arms rise, something feels off. Everything is too quiet, except for the hum of electronics. This place has never been this quiet in the last few weeks. With the outside surveillance that was meticulously installed, there would always be noise. I've always promised myself I would just turn around and leave and reconvene later, when red flags are waving in my face.

I don't have that option, because when I caught sight of Sophia several days ago, she was black and blue. Jax wouldn't let me move up the mission, we didn't have everything in place.

I find the door that goes down to the basement just past the kitchen. Everything is situated perfectly in my bag, so I don't have to spend precious moments looking. I pull out my night vision goggles with a heat sensor and make my way down the rickety steps.

The whole place smells musty, like mildew and water. It's not overwhelming to where I need to breathe only through my mouth, but it is bothersome. The air is cold with a continuous chill. How can someone survive down here?

This is the one area they haven't updated or added anything to. The whole floor is wide open except for a couple of rooms: one for a bathroom and one for storage.

Reaching the bottom, I notice the homemade rapist stand in the corner. There is a bed and a bucket with several thick chains. One of the chains is coming from the dilapidated bed.

Dread fills every cell in my body as I move closer, spotting the unmoving lump on a very thin mattress.

The heat sensor isn't registering anything. My legs move faster. My eyes burn with tears as I shakily pull out a pen light from my cargo pants and take off my night vision goggles, placing them into my backpack.

I pulled back the thin scratchy blanket and looked into the beaten face of Sophia. Her soulless-pleading blue eyes stare at me. The left side of her swollen face carries new and older bruises.

She is laying on her back completely nude. Bruises cover every inch of her previously flawless skin. Blood is dried and crusted over her face, hands and between her legs.

Choking on a sob I realize I'm too late, I've never lost a client. If I just come earlier, this wouldn't have happened. Why did I listen to Jax? From the look of her, she's been dead for several hours.

This revelation snaps me out of my mourning trance. I look around the room. Jared was absolutely in love with Sophia, there's no reason for him to have ended her this fast unless he was tipped off.

I go to another pocket in my cargo pants and pull out my cell phone. Using my fingerprint to turn it on quickly, sending Jax and the rest of the team a message.

Me: Vic is dead. feels like a setup.

Jax: BAB, get out of there now, on our way.

I don't waste any more time than I have to. I cover up Sophia with the thin blanket and whisper 'sorry'.

I don't even bother with the night vision. Using my penlight, I hastily make my way back the way I came.

6

Still remaining quiet, because if this is a setup, I sure as shit am not going to help them know my location, even though they probably already do.

I'm small with my five-foot-seven, hundred-and-twenty-pound frame, but fast and stealthy. I'll be able to get back out in under half the time.

This isn't a rescue operation anymore. Now they're just coming for her body. *M.E.T* will not head up the operation. The New York police will be contacted.

Right when I step foot into the kitchen, several overly bright lights flick on, temporarily blinding me. I screech to a halt, my boots slightly sliding on the expensive marble floor.

"Ms. Moretti you're looking gorgeous as usual." The creepy fuck slowly looks over my body.

Jared is blocking my exit standing right in front of the door on my right-hand side. On my left are three steroid brick-stacked looking fuckers.

"Mr. Cooper, you are looking crazier than ever. How did you know I would be here?" I sneer at him. Jared Cooper III is the laziest Cooper of all of them, we actually went to school together. The first Cooper struck it rich in the oil boom earlier in the 1900s. This Cooper is a dirty creep that's been mooching off his family's money ever since he was born, never contributing to the pot. His father was a great man, he was good friends with my father.

Jax set up security measures for all of us. There are buttons on my phone that are strategically placed in a certain order, that once pushed sends a message directly to him. With my hand hidden in a roomy pocket of my pants, I'm able to push the button that says 'help'. We have other buttons that he could program on here but that's the only one he insisted I have for now.

Other crew members have: 'send team,' and 'stay away.' These are the ones the guys needed the most. It's easier and safer than trying to open the text app and typing out a message.

Jared just shakes his head at me I knew he wouldn't answer. He turns his attention to his men and gives a nod. This is the first time tonight I've felt real fear.

I even my breathing and try not to freak out. I know my brothers and the team are on their way. They probably won't make it here in time, but if I panic, I'm as good as dead.

The two cement blocks grab me by the arms on each side, one of them purposely presses his hand against the side of my breast. The third one stands behind me rubbing his hand over my ass out of view from Jared.

I groan inwardly, knowing what I have to do. I urge the tears to come as I imagine Sophia downstairs. It's a horrible thing, but I need to concentrate on saving myself now. "Please Jared, d-don't do this," I make myself stutter for added effect.

Jared's soulless eyes light up as sleazy smile takes over his face. "I love hearing you beg, hopefully you will do more of it for me later." He's wanted me since grade school. Hitting on me for years, finally, in high school, I realized being nice wasn't going to cut it. I kicked him in the balls helping to get my point across. He left me alone after that. Even though I think my brothers paid him a visit.

My hands squeeze into fists, but I quickly let them go. I don't want the goons holding my arms to realize I tensed up.

I sob, looking down at the floor letting my dark almost black hair form a curtain around my face. There are no tears but it's not hard to make sobbing noises. Being the only girl, I've been able to master this, I should get an award with a red carpet, movie stars and shit.

The goons relax their tight hold on me. I can easily yank both arms free. I take a second to smile, letting my sob taper down, adding some tremors and shaking for effect.

The man behind me, still using my body to block himself from Jared and the other two behemoth wastes-of-space, are none the wiser. His hand moves away from my ass as he presses it flat to my back. He pushes his meaty fingers straight down between my underwear and skin.

Right after Jared, he's the one I want to kill the most. I can hear him lightly groaning as he squeezes the round globe of my ass. He presses himself flush against my back, letting me feel how hard I've made him. I almost laugh out loud, thinking steroids have depleted his stubby nub.

Focus Anna.

There's no time like the present. I don't want to wait until his fingers start moving down more. He's close enough to where I can feel his sticky-hot breath on my neck.

I push up to my tippy toes, slamming my head back hard on the bridge of his nose. The move takes all the men by surprise, causing the other two idiots to let go of me.

"Fucking bitch, you broke my nose." He screams as the sticky blood sprays on my exposed neck and on the back of my head, coating my hair in red. I can feel it heavy and thick, nothing bleeds more than a nose.

With my right hand, I quickly grab my knife that's still sheathed on the inside of my thigh and stab the guy to the right in his bulging neck, then yanking it back out. I can hear him gurgling, gasping for breath with a faint hiss of air leaving his body. He quickly drops down to his knees falling to his side. He turns several shades lighter as his hands try desperately to keep the life inside of him.

I notice the blood surrounding the man like a dam broke, and the thick red liquid is flowing freely, forever tarnishing the glossy floors. My fighting back was not expected. I only have several more seconds before the rest leap into action.

With my knife still in my right hand, I drop down

into a squat position. During a fight when someone tries to grab you, they assume that you will still be standing up.

Tossing the knife to my left hand, I stab the other stone block right in the thigh hitting an artery, feeling my serrated edge knife scrape along the bone.

The guy howls out in pain, which makes me chuckle. No more scary tanks, just grown men literally crying.

My knife is stuck in his leg, most likely around bone and muscle. I quickly stand with my legs spread apart. I can hear the guy behind me getting closer as a seething Jared runs right at me.

It only takes one blow of my fist to his pasty face to slow him down, as the bone cracks under my knuckles. Blood, just like the guy behind, me sprays everywhere. Jared instantly grabs his face and stills.

I squat again to grab the smaller knife hidden in my boot. Standing up as agonizing pain tears through my left side, causing bright white lights to dance vividly in my vision. I have just enough in me to swing around and stab the bloodied-broken nose man in the gut with my knife, silently praying he drops out of commission.

Both of us dropped down at the same time, it looks as though we floated gracefully, leaving only Jared standing. I quickly embrace my side with both hands. Blood is oozing between my fingers and pooling underneath me. *This is so not good.*

The stone statue on the floor next to me stops

moving and has turned white, ghost white. Jared is slowly moving towards me, making sure I don't have any other weapons. If I had the strength, I would pretend to pull something out.

He suddenly stops, I can see his expensive loafer's moving through my distorted haze. His feet turn around quickly, running in the other direction. Droplets of blood trickling after him, making a trail so he can't get away.

That's when I can hear the sound he ran from; the front door being kicked down.

Jax is in a full run towards me as he drops to his knees sliding like I'm home base. Ray Sanchez and my brother, Colt, kneel down on my other side. My brother, Finn, also kneels down looking scared. Ray looks at me with sadness in his eyes as he holds my petite hand with his enormous one. He is one of the hundreds of guys employed by my family.

Jax yells to a couple of other guys, I'm not sure who they are and points to the back of the house where Jared made his escape.

"Don't worry sis, you are far too stubborn for anything to happen to you." Finn coos to me as he starts to cut off my shirt. I try to look around, but a cloud of darkness slowly fills my eyes, eventually taking over.

No more pain, and no more light.

CHAPTER 2

*a*nna
3 Months Later

Grabbing my keys off a handcrafted table my father made next to the front door, I run my fingertips over the intricate wood. Letting the memories of times past play like an old projection wheel through my mind.

The cabin I've claimed as my own for the past three months is in a very small town called Mountainside, about twenty miles north of Aspen. It belongs to the Moretti family.

I can envision my mother radiating light and happiness as she sways through the front door. Making each of us feel like the most important person in her world. Her dark almost black hair shines, flowing against her back, as her emerald eyes sparkle with laughter.

My parents originally thought of buying a property

in Aspen, but according to them and I quote, 'there are just too many rich snobs there.'

After coming here several times a year, it never fazes any of us when we run into a celebrity. They're here for the same reasons we are, peace and quiet.

The cabin was hand built with giant logs. Back in the '60s, a grieving widow built this place for the love of his life, where he spent the rest of his life peacefully alone as one with nature. Townsfolk said he would always talk to her like she never even left, *maybe the place is haunted.* She did leave though, right into the arms of another man.

Hardwood flooring was placed throughout. Everything is original, even the expensive handcrafted wooden furniture. It doesn't scream 60's, it screams rugged nature.

Heading into the garage, silently praying that my old Jeep, *Wilma,* will actually start. My mom started this tradition with naming all of our vehicles and we continue to do so. Colt, my more than likely STD infected brother, always comes up with what he calls badass names like reaper, dragon ass, skull bone. Stupid shit like that.

It takes several cranks before my baby finally purrs to life. It's January in Colorado and cold as hell. Last week we received eighteen inches of snow, half of it remains.

I switch the radio to my favorite station. *"... Thank you for joining us for Aspen at eight. In our top news, this morning Johnny Sinclair age four, was taken by his noncus-todial parent, Patrick Sinclair. Patrick is considered armed and dangerous, putting Johnny in a dire situation..."* I turn up the radio some.

When the Amber alerts started, we always paid close attention. You never know when you could be in the right place, at the right time, and it also comes with the job. *"... Johnny has light blonde hair with brown eyes. He was last seen wearing dark blue Spiderman pajamas. If you have any information please call your local authorities..."*

I make a mental note just as a precaution. I imagine the father and Johnny to be long gone by now.

The main street in Aspen is deserted, it's been this way since the snowstorm and insane cold visited. We haven't been above freezing in over a month. We hover right around ten degrees.

The general store only has five cars, at least two of them are for the workers. *Aspen General* is about a third in size of a major store. The building is professionally done; shaded in dark browns, giving it an outdoor feel.

Taking my time through the aisles, I imagine I'll be in here for at least an hour. I only need to get maybe a weeks' worth of food for one person. I left New York three months ago, here it's peaceful and relaxing compared to the insurmountable stress there.

Moving down the aisle, I hum a song my mom used to sing to us as I look through the different cans of soup. *I like shopping, I just suck at cooking.*

Glancing down the aisle, I freeze in my tracks. I can

see Chad Holmes talking to Peggy Stevens. She is our local church lady and the one person in town that's in everybody's business, don't get me wrong she's sweet as hell I just dislike the gossip and the meddling.

I slowly back up and get out of the aisle, it's not just Peggy I'm avoiding, it's Chad, too. He's been flirting hard and coming on strong ever since I got here three months ago. Chad is a thirty-five-year-old that runs his family's hardware store. The nicest man I've ever met, not really my type-very lanky and out of shape. If for some reason we ever do get together, I can imagine how surprised he would be with what I do for a living.

Chad starts to head in my direction, I don't think he spotted me yet, but I need to get away. I'm not above hiding in the bathroom or in the employee break room until he vacates the store.

Whipping around I start to jog. Around the next aisle, I run straight into a basket being handled by big meaty hands, calloused but manicured hands, deadly gorgeous hands.

My foolishness sends the strangers basket plowing into a display shelf right in front of us. Thankfully nothing comes down.

"I am so sorry," I haven't had a chance to take in the features of the abused stranger. I'm too nervous watching the shelf, there have to be at least two-hundred cans stacked up there. I slowly envision them crashing to the ground. The real question is would I stay, or would I run.

I can hear it now, "*idiot cleanup on aisle five...*"

"Again, I am so sor..." I say as I slowly look up. Well hello, *holy shit.*

I did not expect to almost kill a freaking Adonis. My eyes traveled down to his brown boots and start to work my way back up. Most jeans have seams and creases in them. Some of them you can even tell they're a little bit big. Not this guy, every square inch fills out, there's not a seam or a crease in sight. This guy is packing illegal muscles under there.

He's currently stretching with his hands over his head. Either he's being vain or just needs to stretch. His shirt rides up with his arms, exposing his low hanging jeans plus a glorious sliver of black from his boxers. The bottom of his perfectly sculpted abs peek through. He has to have an eight pack. *I wonder if they have ten and twelve packs?*

His black Henley sweatshirt fits snugly to his lickable skin. Every part of him is muscled, it looks like even his fingers are jacked up.

I know by looking in his eyes many panties have burned or just disintegrated. *I sound cheesy but damn.* The lightest and whitest blue I've ever seen, like the ocean, decided to fuck the clouds one day and that's where he got his eyes. I snort out a small giggle before I go back molesting him with my eyes. *God, I'm a creep!*

His face is the epitome of a godlike creature, carved bone structure that must have been worshipped to create his glowing skin.

I can't even believe that I'm thinking this, maybe I'm incredibly shallow, but who the fuck isn't?

His fuck me lips turn into an amused smirk as he can see me ogling him. I would more likely call it observing. *God get a grip, Anna.*

His deep voice vibrates straight through me, my nipples instantly peak in delight, heat explodes in my core. "It looks like you were running from something or someone."

I glance down to see what I wore today exhaling a sigh of relief that at least I'm not in my pajamas. I have a pair of leggings with my black designer snow boots that go up to my knees. I don't care too much for bulky coats and jackets so I'm just wearing a *Broncos* sweatshirt I got for Christmas.

My dark hair is expertly pushed up into a black beanie, no reason to brush it this morning.

"Yeah, there is someone I didn't want to talk to." I hang my head down feeling like shit for saying that. It is kind of rude to avoid people. I glance in his direction, then quickly look back towards the cans, he's taking his time checking me out, too. Inwardly smiling, I want to make sure that they're not about to topple over.

"So, are you new in town? My name is Anna and I live over in Mountainside." I stretch out my unmanicured hand.

The Adonis squeezes but not too hard. He doesn't shake my hand he brings it up and kisses my knuckles.

Oh swoon. "My name is Maxim. I just bought a house up there a couple of months ago. It's very nice to meet you, Anna." He doesn't let go of my hand.

I pull it free as we both start to make our way towards the cashier. I don't even feel like shopping anymore, I just want to get out of here.

"Well, it's nice to meet you, too, neighbor." I smile as he goes to the next checkout aisle over.

The place is empty we both finish around the same time and head out together. I never had problems flirting with men but for some reason, this guy is making me hellaciously nervous.

Maxim walks over to my car after unloading his groceries and leans his back against it, "would you li..."

His eyes widen in alarm as he grabs my shoulders and pushes me hard towards the back of my Jeep.

I land painfully on my ass, but that doesn't even faze me as I watch the old Ford truck, skid and screech to a stop two inches from where I was standing.

I get up slowly and wipe the cold harsh powder from my bum as Maxim stands next to me. We both watch as Mrs. Jenkins, eighty-two year's old, finds her glasses and puts them back on her face. She gets out of her truck easily, then slowly walks towards the store, ignorant to what just happened.

Moving closer to me tucking a tendril of hair behind my ear, "this is not usually the way I meet new people. Especially gorgeous women." Maxim states and I awkwardly laugh. He is right next to me, all I want to do is put my head on his chest and inhale deeply.

"Yeah, that's an understatement." We both stand there for several minutes, it was probably only ten seconds.

Maxim gets a call and waves goodbye to me. His eyes never leave mine, they follow me. He watches me drive down Main Street until he disappears from view.

For twenty years I have trained mentally and physically. I let myself down in a big way. It didn't hit me till much later that I noticed several black SUV's that seem very out of place at a small town, almost deserted grocery store. I will also never let myself live down the men I saw in the store, that only seemed noticeable when I got close to Maxim.

I was too busy flirting and ogling the strange man instead of doing what I was supposed to do, trained to do. I know I would've gone home had I seen all this, *then I might not have gotten myself in a life or death position.*

CHAPTER 3

*a*nna

I moan rolling over trying to swat my alarm that's beeping, hopefully into the wall, so it shatters. It is way too early to be going off. I find my phone, it's not the alarm that's going off its dead silent no vibrations. *What the hell woke me up?*

I wrestle my sticky eyelids open. Yeah, I'm the type that doesn't do mornings gracefully or beautiful. Outside, I can hear a man grunt and continually yell 'fuck'. He sounds like he's in pain. I throw the covers back, revolting when my feet hit the ice-cold floor. We have heated floors in this cabin, but I've never used them before. I make a mental note to figure it out later.

I tiptoe to my window, I'm not trying to be quiet, I just don't want my feet to freeze and fall off. I look out the window and I can see a man clenching his left hand with his right. *Somebody must have bought the Kipling place.*

His back is towards me, but I can see blood dripping on the ground and what looks like a discarded nail gun. Shit, this guy needs help. The dripping is faster than a leaky faucet.

I run downstairs throwing my boots on before opening the front door. I walk towards my new next-door neighbor. Not the best way to meet somebody with a nail in the hand. Shivering, I realize my dumb ass forgot to grab a coat.

Dammit, I'm in a tank top and I don't have a bra on. This is really not the best way to meet your neighbor. I can't run back to the house; this guy could be in trouble. Another mental note: wear a bra 24/7, *yeah right*!

Walking up next to the guy, I hear the crunch of frozen snow under my boots. Each property has several acres of land, I'm lucky his is not one of the bigger ones.

The Kipling's haven't lived here since the 1970s. Mr. and Mrs. Kipling both passed away in this house. They were in their nineties. The property has been transferred down the family line, but nothing's ever been done with it, nobody ever visits.

Every year since the 70s, numerous offers have been put on this place, but they were all refused. I imagine the family not wanting to sell, it's a beautiful property, even though it's gone to shit. Plus, the story behind it is more tear jerking... the couple had been married for sixty years and died peacefully together. Not sure how they died, most likely just from old age. The wife went, then husband right after.

One guy twenty years ago, offered double the market value, he still received a big fat no. They had companies that would take care of the lawn in the summer and the snow in the winter, but nobody to take care of the actual house.

It's about half the size of ours and has more of a cottage feel instead of a cabin. White paint is peeling off the deck and the siding. It would be great for a grandparents place.

I gasp, my eyes open big like saucers as Maxim turns to look at me holding his injured hand. "You live here? Did you buy the Kipling place?"

He nods, grimacing. I sigh, realizing that it's better to talk later. My eyes come back to focus on his face instead of his injured hand. Maxim is staring at me, though not at my face but my chest. I look down at my thin tank top and my nipples are the hardest they've ever been. You can even make out my areola. I curse myself I should've put on a freaking coat.

Covering my chest with one arm, I grab his forearm leading us back to my house.

Neither one of us says anything. All we do is listen to the quietness of the mountains and the crunching of our feet through the snow.

Stepping inside, my boots are kicked off. I point Maxim over to the kitchen area. Quickly, I run up to the stairs and throw on a pair of socks and sweater, the same one I wore yesterday when I first met him.

I start looking through all the bathroom cabinets hoping to find the medical kit I know we have some-where. My brother Finn's a doctor and he likes to keep supplies everywhere we go.

Finally, in the master bathroom, I find it. I stay in one of the guest bedrooms, Jax usually occupies the master bedroom.

Quickly walking down to the kitchen, I can feel the cold of the hardwood floors through my socks. That is what I'm doing today even if it takes all day learning this heated floor shit. It's probably just a button I push somewhere. I could call my brothers and ask, but they would expect that. I need to start learning this stuff on my own. I can take down four men, but I can't figure out how to get the heated floors to work.

Maxim is standing over the sink, clutching his hand, letting the blood drip there instead of all over the counters and floor.

"You should go to the hospital."

He shakes his head no, "no hospitals, I can't stand them."

I sigh, looking up at the ceiling for a second, "how do you expect us to get that nail out of your hand?"

He looks amused while he smirks, "with pliers. Do you have any?"

Is he serious? "Are you serious? I won't be able to pull that nail out of your hand."

"I'll do it, all you have to do is stand there and look gorgeous. Can you get me a pair?" Wow, he's laying it on thick. Smiling I know he's trying to distract me from the situation.

It takes me about twenty minutes to find a pair of pliers. I happen to find the heavy-duty kind. I'm really gonna have to learn my way around this place. I don't have the slightest clue where anything is. I don't like feeling helpless.

I help Maxim hold his hand down as he tightly grips the end of the nail with the pliers. It takes several minutes before he gets it out. During that time, he would grunt and swear.

I can handle the blood and I can help if needed, but I just don't have the strength, that nail was embedded through his freaking hand.

We both look at the slim piece of metal as he drops it on the counter it's caked in blood. His hand has started bleeding more once the obstruction was removed. It's a little fascinating I've never seen a nail go through a freaking body part. I've seen a knife go in somebody, I've put them in several people. Maybe I should switch to nail guns?

Not to sound stupid, but I want to ask him if he can put it up towards the light. I wonder if it's true, if we actually see a hole going through, maybe a small beam of light will shine back at us.

I shake off that thought with a chuckle. Maxim just looks at me not saying anything, he probably thinks

I'm crazy.

I carefully grab his injured hand and put it under the running water, rinsing off all the blood and dirt. It doesn't look like something went through, it just looks like he's got a little tiny hole on each side.

I'm a little bit worried if he has any damage. "Maxim, I think you should go to the doctor. What if you hit bone, ligaments or even tendons? We have no idea what damage could be done."

He puts his arm around my shoulder pulling me close into a hug, "thank you for helping me. I'm not too worried, this is my left hand, my non-dominant hand. If for some reason it gets worse, I promise you I'll go to the doctor." I inhale his wonderfully toxic scent a little louder than I should have. Thankfully he doesn't acknowledge my weirdness. He smells divine, like sweat, wood and nature.

I smile a smile that makes me feel a little better. Dumping the antiseptic on his hand causes him to hiss. His teeth are clenched together so tightly, I'm afraid he might break his jaw.

The bleeding has slowed as gauze is wrapped around his hand followed by an ace bandage.

When we're done, Maxim turns to look at me. He just stares for several seconds, I lick my bottom lip in anticipation. My mouth feels too dry. His right hand comes up as his thumb moves over my bottom lip.

"Thank you for helping me. I haven't used a nail

gun for years." His right-hand moves down and grabs mine, lightly squeezing.

"I could tell," I say as we walk over to the dining room table. "So, you're my new neighbor, huh?"

He smirks, "how 'bout that."

"I'm curious how you were able to get the Kipling's to sell their place?" I watch him curiously.

"My family's been wanting a cabin in the mountains for a while, nothing big like yours, just a place we can come and relax. We just made an offer they couldn't refuse." He moves his chair closer to mine and grabs my hand lightly massaging my palm with his thumb.

My body involuntarily shivers as my nipple peak again. I'm relieved that I'm wearing a sweater so he can't see. Just being this close to him is such a turn on.

I don't have very much experience with guys. It's practically nonexistent. I have four overprotective brothers and a father; my sex life is nil, even though I'm twenty-three years old.

I can't tell if Maxim notices my response to him or he's just really good at hiding it.

Maxim moves my hair off my shoulder and is whispering in my ear. I can feel his hot breath tingling the skin on my neck. It takes everything I have to keep from straddling him. "Let me make dinner for you tonight. I would like to pay you back for helping me and I want to spend more time with you."

I don't even know what I should say. This guy reeks of danger and I'm supposed to be here getting over the botched job I did three months ago. Getting my head back in the game.

My mouth answers before my brain can catch up, "I would love that."

I need to separate myself from him before I jump in his lap. I get up and head over to the sink to start cleaning the mess we made from his injury.

"Where's your bathroom?" This house is kind of big, so I turn around to take him there.

He grabs my hand, slipping his fingers between mine as we walk. It feels nice and comfortable.

After he goes in, I head back towards the kitchen and spend the next ten minutes cleaning. Finished, I start to wonder if he's okay, he's been gone a while.

Waiting for him at the table, I don't want to be intrusive or annoying. Right as I sit down, he walks back out.

"Are you okay?"

Maxim studies me for a second before answering, "I was actually looking for pain reliever. My hand and my head are starting to throb."

"Oh." He moves towards me and pulls me up into a standing position.

"I'll be back later, I can't wait to see you tonight." He pushes my hair off my shoulder, I've noticed he loves doing this, then grabs the back of my head with his good hand.

Maxim looks between my eyes and my mouth. I

instinctively lick my lips. Is he going to kiss me? *Please kiss me.*

Bending his head down, he lightly kisses the edges of my mouth. I can barely feel him moving his lips over mine. He pulls back and looks at me. He must get the reaction he wanted because he softly presses his mouth to mine, sweeping his tongue over my bottom lip.

He removes himself from me, pulling back before I get a chance to react. "I'll see you tonight." His voice is full of lust and need. I just nod with my mouth open. God that was hot.

I watch Maxim's squeezable tight ass in jeans as he walks away. Once the door clicks shut, I plop down at the kitchen table inhaling a deep breath.

"Holy shit," I say to no one.

CHAPTER 4

*M*axim

I close the door to the dilapidated piece of shit cottage I bought and lean my back against the old wooden door. My head falls back as I look up at the ceiling, I keep telling myself it's not too late to bring in reinforcements somebody else can handle this job for me.

My hand is throbbing, but I've been in worse pain, this is a walk in the park, and my dick is the size of a rocket ready for takeoff. I've never been this hard before not even with Gina.

With Anna, I have a love-hate relationship. Don't get me wrong, I'm still going to kill her but there's just something about this woman. Maybe if I would have met her under different circumstances, one that didn't involve revenge.

I just finished cleaning up my mess of tools outside. I've only barely started working on this place, the whole nail in the hand thing was a gimmick. Yes, I did shoot myself in the fucking hand with a nail gun for a reason. I highly doubted that Anna would be as approachable to me if I went over and asked for a cup of sugar. I needed to get into her house with her fawning all over me.

And it worked fucking wonders, now I got a dinner date scheduled for tonight and I had access to her house for over ten minutes.

At first, I was only trying to be loud and obscenely annoying. Who doesn't hate when somebody starts working on their house at the crack of dawn, not Anna? That woman slept through two hours of me doing manual labor and I was not quiet.

The idea came to me after two hours with no signs of life from her. At first, I was going to lay my hand against the wood, but I didn't want it to get stuck there, then I wouldn't have access into her house. She would be sitting there trying to help me figure out how to get my hand unmanned from the wall. But, knowing my luck she probably would've slept through the whole damn thing, then I would have been stuck there.

My backup plan was, if she didn't wake up, I was going to pound on the neighbor's door needing help, spewing off some shit about a dead phone. I mean you really can't drive yourself to the hospital with a nail in your hand, well I could. I drove to the hospital with a bullet in my gut and a knife in my shoulder, but I'm not normal. Of course, I would never go to the hospital for that.

I touched the part of my hand that's covered in gauze. She did it so carefully, making sure not to hurt me anymore. If she only knew who I really was and how much I'm going to hurt her. How much I'm going to destroy her.

I storm up to my shower, this is the one room that was done right away. If you want to be clean, you got to make sure the place you're getting clean in, is clean.

Common sense understands that I shouldn't be getting my hand or the dressing wet, but on a lighter note, I did make sure that the nail was clean before I shot it right in the middle of my palm.

The feeling as it entered my hand was more euphoric than painful.

I've got to get her out of my damn head. I had to leave right away, or I would have bent her sweet ass over that damn table where she cleaned and bandaged me. In my family, I don't even blink an eye as I drain the life from some little miserable soul, but I do draw the line at rape and anything that has to do with children.

In my colder than shit shower, I leave my injured left hand away from the water as much as I possibly can, letting the cool water cascade over my overheated body. My right-hand slides down my tight stomach and over the edge of my thighs, gripping then tugging my never-ending hard-on.

This little bastard has a mind of his own and doesn't plan on going down anytime soon. Closing my eyes, I imagine Anna and the little tank top she was wearing that left nothing to the imagination.

I cursed the cold when I first got up this morning, it was actually a blessing, peaking her impressive tits. I stroke harder and faster, twisting just right.

I imagined Anna slowly pulling her barely-there tank top off, showing me what I need and want. My body's tense, I'm so close.

She dips both her fingers in her mouth sucking on them matching my thrusts, she trails them down right between her palm-sized boobs leaving a wet trail. She glides over her stomach, down to her navel. Eventually connecting with the sexy landing strip right above her pussy.

The sultry woman who one day I will wrap my hands around her throat and watch as the life vanishes from her eyes, slides her fingers through her slit spreading them, letting me see her arousal. Her thighs are wet from her juices, she pushes two fingers inside of her matching my tempo.

My body tenses and grows tighter, I'm jackhammering my cock up and down. Anna drops to her knees, opening her mouth on a moan, ready to collect all of me.

My load explodes, shooting forward multiple

streams of hot sticky come that lasts almost a minute and paints the tiles of my shower.

Some of my edginess has worn off and I'm feeling better, this raging hard-on won't go away until I finally dip inside of her.

When I left her to clean the kitchen, I planted several bugs, normally something like this would only take me a few minutes. However, this family and their business know what to look for and where to look for it, so I had to step up my game.

One of my vendors, fucking overweight guy, was able to get me the newest innovative up-and-coming listening devices.

These little fuckers cost five thousand dollars apiece and they are 99% untraceable and invisible to the naked eye.

I was able to plant them in almost every room including the living room and the kitchen. Those two were the hardest, Anna was around the whole time. I slipped one underneath the dining room table it shouldn't be noticeable unless somebody crawls under there spotting a tiny black dot.

My plan has been working beautifully so far, and it won't be long until everything goes into action. Patience is everything at this point. Even being several weeks ahead of schedule. I figured it would take longer to casually run into her.

I decide to work in the kitchen for the rest of the

day. I want to keep my mind off Anna and the rest of my shitty existence.

"*Soon, Anna, soon,*" I say as I grab a picture of me and the woman I'll never see again, due to the Moretti's.

CHAPTER 5

*A*nna

Maxim has been working on his house for a couple of hours now. I thought for sure he would stay inside and rest his hand, maybe do something less invigorating?

I've been watching from the living room window. I actually had the audacity to go and drag a chair, planting it right in front of the living room window.

The whole southside of our wall is floor to ceiling in glass. But luckily for me, I know that people cannot see in the windows when the sun is brightly shining. It creates a glare. *Creeper much?*

I wonder if he thinks I'm watching him, maybe he can feel me. It's like that old saying when people can feel they're being watched but they can't see anyone. The back of their neck hairs stand on end or their arms cover in goosebumps.

An hour ago, Maxim took off his coat. The chill is still bitter with a harsh cold bite since it's only January, but the sun is out giving us a reprieve from Mother Nature's winter.

He has on a black Henley sweatshirt that's glued to his body. It fits every curve and crevice, molding and outlining his hardened muscles. Occasionally it lifts up, teasing me with a peak of his defined stomach.

It's got to be in the forties out there, but Maxim is working hard building up a sweat. Maybe I should be neighborly and take him over some lemonade or something. Giving me a chance to be closer to him.

Every now and then, he'll turn and look back towards the house. I find myself wishing for cloud coverage, so he could see me sitting here, then he'll realize I'm a total creeper and not even come over tonight.

What is it about this man?

I slowly slide my hand into my black leggings. I discarded my tank top earlier and opted for a heavy sweater.

I figured out the heated floors earlier, but the mountain chill still settles through me. My frame doesn't appreciate winter at all.

Dipping my fingers in my panties I barely graze the top of my clit when someone starts pounding on my front door.

My head snaps in that direction then I quickly look back, Maxim is still outside working. Who the hell is here? I quickly push the recliner back in place, nobody needs to see what I was doing.

I rub my hardened peaks trying to get them to subside before I open the front door. These suckers are stiff, and I can barely make them out through the thick sweater.

As soon as the door opens my brother Colt rushes in, grabbing me in a bear hug swinging me around.

I scream while laughing, "Colt, let me down!"

He laughs as he tightens his bear hug hold on me. "I missed you baby girl."

Colt moves back as Jax steps into his space. My oldest brother wraps me in a tight, fatherly embrace that makes my eyes burn.

He steps back cradling my face in his hands, "how are you?"

I quickly blink away the wetness in the back of my eyes and nod my head, "I'm good, really good, actually being here has helped a lot," I lie.

Jax scrutinizes my face, knowing I'm not being honest, but I don't want to rehash things and worry them further. I just want to spend this time with my brothers.

I move away from him and walk towards the kitchen. I can see them giving each other a knowing look right before I turn around. I know that look, I created that damn look. They know I'm not okay.

When we reach the kitchen, I turn around with a raised eyebrow, "What are you two doing here?" They both just stare at me, maybe they wanted to ease into the conversation. "Not that I mind it. You both rarely ever leave New York unless it's a big job." Now everything clicks. "So, what's the big job?"

"A senator that has a vacation home in Aspen really enjoys his time with the company of younger boys." Colt clenches his teeth as he tells me.

"That's disgusting," I hiss, I can't stand pedophiles.

"We'll be staying at St Regis in Aspen if you need us. We would like to hang out though, maybe after this job is done. We've got several days of surveillance ahead of us." Jax looks at me hopefully, an expression that's rarely ever seen on him.

Everyone says that we all look the same, with our lightly tanned skin, very dark almost black hair, and green eyes.

Colt is designed like a tank; built and thick, he works out several hours every day. Jax looks deadly. Out of all of us, he's the one people fear the most.

Jax takes on all the deadly and dangerous cases. He doesn't want that on the rest of our conscience. He stands an inch taller than Colt at 6'3". At thirty years old, he's the big brother of us five siblings.

We always give him shit for being so old, but he doesn't look it, not in the least, he spends maybe a couple of hours in the gym. Training and sparring takes most of his time. Out of all my brothers, he's the only one I've never been able to beat, ever.

Jax has a strong build but not overly muscular like

Colt, he prefers guns. I prefer knives, I always have one with me. Colt just prefers his fists, he even uses his legs to get somebody in a vice grip. He can snap the neck on someone in two seconds flat.

Two of our brothers are missing today, it would've been great to see everyone. Mason is the second oldest, helps when needed but he'd rather be investing and dealing with hedge funds. He's recently engaged to Lee and he couldn't be happier, she is his perfect match. He loathes when we call him Wall Street, which we make sure to always do.

Finn is our other brother, he's the only one besides Mason that aspired to do something different. He's a doctor working on his fellowship. He hasn't decided if he wants to stay in the ER or open his own practice.

My father and Jax were pissed at first, they wanted the *M.E.T.* (Moretti Extraction Team) to be primarily family members.

Now they're elated because Finn also helps when we have cases that go bad, some of them are highly classified. When we get to these victims they don't want to be in the spotlight, they're usually famous. Finn will come over and evaluate them, if it's worse than we thought, they'll be transported to the hospital he works at making sure that he's their primary doctor. Finn will make sure of their confidentiality, and that nothing is leaked.

This would have been the case with me, but my brother wasn't able to operate, he was too scared. So, we had to have a close confidant at the hospital do the surgery.

He's fixed broken noses on all of us and several stab wounds.

We have over a hundred operatives working for us. We treat everyone the same and we're always out on missions. None of us want to sit behind a desk, we would rather be in the field. This is the same for Mason, he comes back every now and then to get his itch scratched.

Jax walks over to the bar just off the kitchen grabbing his favorite decanter and three glasses, pouring us two fingers of whiskey.

Shit, he only brings out the good stuff when life's about to get heavy. I don't want to talk about this now, but I know they won't leave me alone until I do. I shift back and forth on my feet, waiting.

After passing them out, we all skim back the burning liquid. Jax and Colt both watch me in silence, *here we go.*

"You need to talk about this, Anna," Jax says in a father-like tone.

"I know, I just don't think I'm ready to yet," I whisper, looking down at the many variations of design in the hardwood floor. *This shit is really detailed wonder why I never looked at it before.*

Colt comes over and wraps his arm around my shoulder, pulling my body close to his. "It wasn't your fault you need to understand that."

"Yes, it was. If I had been there several hours earlier like I was planning to, she would still be alive." I wipe away the single tear that found its way out of my tight hold.

"You need to stop this shit Anna, we've gone over this. That was the designated time that we all agreed upon." Jax growls as he fills his glass all the way to the top. "We planned this shit for weeks, something wasn't right, someone targeted you, and I'm going to figure out who it was." He slams his glass down loud enough to make me jump but not hard enough to break.

Colt squeezes my shoulders, "I think we have a mole. Someone among us ratted us out."

Jax nods his head in agreement, as I shake mine. There's no way that can happen, we are such a tight-knit family business made up of cousins, siblings and loyal operatives.

"Who would do that? That's just not possible." I turn so my body is facing away.

"Anything is possible when money and power are involved. We have lots of enemies." Jax states as he walks towards me using his thumbs to wipe away my tears. "You're going to get through this Anna, everything will work itself out and we will figure out what happened. We have everybody on surveillance. Phones are being tapped and I've hired an outside company to follow those besides the three of us, Finn or Mason."

"Wow, you really believe someone's trying to harm us?" My eyes widen in surprise. I can't believe someone close to us would be doing this. "What if someone was threatened?"

"That could be, but until we know for sure, all cases are secretive, don't give out any information unless it's to the four of us." Jax's voice has lowered now as he talks to me. I love when he's sweet and calm. His temper can shoot off in an instant and I don't want to be the cause of that, or have it focused on me.

This revelation stuns me more than anything. I didn't even realize they were thinking this. I just thought I fucked up big-time, but if there is somebody that's trying to hurt us, this could be dangerous for all of us, even deadly.

I sit down at the dining room table as Jax goes and grabs all of us a bottle of water. They still have about a half an hour drive to Aspen.

They both hug me goodbye, and as soon as the door closes the tears run free. Like a damn that's been building and building for years. The pressure of the water was too much, and it just gave away. Here comes the flood.

A knock pulls me from my pity party. I really should've checked my face before I opened the door, because it prompted the delivery man to mildly freak out, asking if he needed to call 911.

I laughed it off and told him my monthly cycle had started. I've never seen anyone get away from me that fast before. My eyes felt like they were swollen. I know they're red and puffy. The poor guy probably thought I took a beating.

Putting the dozen white roses on the kitchen island, fear and annoyance take over. This is the thirtieth anonymous package I've received in the last one and a half years.

I open the card, realizing I will never appreciate white roses again.

You will look so good when you wear white for me.

There is never a signature. I toss the beautiful roses in the trash after taking a picture, then make my way to my room pulling out the box hidden under my jeans in my dresser.

No one knows about my stalker/secret admirer/pain in the ass. In case something ever happens to me, I kept all the previous cards, with a picture of the gift, if there is one, stapled together. I make sure to write the date on the back when it arrived.

I've received a lot of flowers, lingerie, pictures of myself and family at different venues. The one that creeped me out the most was when I was on a job. There is no way they could've known unless they were on the inside.

I should let my brothers know, but I feel like an idiot holding onto the info for this long.

I have a bad feeling very soon everything will connect and just blow up.

The bad feeling starts to grow and fester. I take the box and head into the cabin office. I quickly package up the disturbing items and leave a note for my New York doorman to put it in my apartment.

I'm not taking a chance. If something were to happen to me, my brothers would be able to find this and hopefully piece everything together.

CHAPTER 6

*M*axim
 There's nothing like manual labor to get your blood flowing to ease your conscience and to make everything seem worthwhile.

I STAND BACK AND ADMIRE THE WORK THAT I SPENT THE last several hours on. All the wood siding on this cottage needs to be replaced. I managed to get one side of the house done and that's only because I didn't dick around.

Of course, this happened to be the easiest side with no windows or obstructions to interfere, just me the wood and my saw.

. . .

MY MEN HAVE ASKED ME SEVERAL TIMES IF I WOULD LIKE them to take over. They know they need to remain hidden and out of sight. I currently have twenty guys outside with me, and they have blended into their environment. Anna or any of the other neighbors farther away will never know they are here.

THERE ARE FIVE INSIDE THE HOUSE. I ALWAYS TAKE A BIG group of trained guards with me. I can fight better than any of them, but several times I've had to go against multiple men that were ordered to kill me.

ONE TIME I ALMOST DIDN'T MAKE IT. NO MORE chances, I don't need to prove anything to myself anymore. It's all about survival now. You don't get this high up without others trying to take everything from you.

NO MOVEMENT OR NOISE HAS COME FROM NEXT DOOR, I wonder if Anna's even home. I hope she's still looking forward to tonight. For some reason, we have an unobtainable attraction between us.

JUMPING IN THE SHOWER I QUICKLY WASH THE DAY AWAY. I still have a few hours before dinner tonight. I need to make some kind of plan of what I'm going to do and what I want to accomplish. Well I know what my end result will be, but the steps to get there is a process.

ANNA'S EXTREMELY SHELTERED EXISTENCE IS WORKING towards my advantage, making it easier for me to slip in. She's been craving a close physical connection to somebody else other than then males in her life.

I SMILE, I'VE BEEN CRAVING THAT CLOSE PHYSICAL connection with her, too. Too bad it won't last for long, it can't.

EARLIER, A BLACK SUV DROVE DOWN THE STREET, NOT one of mine, Anna and I are the only two houses this far down. They weren't here for me.

I QUICKLY GET DRESSED AFTER MY SHOWER AND GRAB myself a bite to eat before settling into my dilapidated office.

I MANAGED TO MAKE A MAKESHIFT DESK USING A TABLE and an old chair that I found down in the basement.

. . .

WHILE MY LAPTOP TURNS ON I DIG INTO MY MEAGER meal of a ham sandwich and tomato soup. This is one of my mom's go-to meals that she always gave me and my siblings.

I REMEMBER HER ALWAYS SAYING LIFE'S ABOUT EXPLORING and having fun, why waste it cleaning the house and cooking constantly.

THAT'S WHAT MY FATHER ALWAYS BELIEVED THE CHEF and the maid were for, he would do anything for my mom, even cook and clean himself.

AFTER THE HEADPHONES ARE PLACED ON MY EARS, I rewind the recorded audio back to when I first saw the SUV pull up.

JAX'S VOICE FILLS MY HEADSET. I STAND AND START TO pace, looking back at the screen. Fuck, why didn't I install video surveillance, too? I listen to them talk back and forth, meaningless shit.

"IT WASN'T YOUR FAULT, YOU NEED TO UNDERSTAND THAT."

. . .

"*Yes, it was. If I had been there several hours earlier like I was planning to, she would still be alive.*" Anna pleads.

"*You need to stop this shit Anna, we've gone over this. That was the designated time that we all agreed upon.*" I hear Jax growl. "*We planned this shit for weeks, something wasn't right, someone targeted you, and I'm going to figure out who it was.*" Something slams down hard on the table.

A voice I don't recognize chimes in, "*I think we have a mole. Someone among us ratted us out.*"

This is more information that I've had about any of the jobs that they've done. I rip the headset from my ears and throw it across the room watching it break.

My breathing is erratic now as I open and close my fist at my side, I'm stomping across the den of my office like a perturbed child.

Looking back on this, I would almost be afraid that I was just going to break through the floor. I'm not lightly stomping, I'm stomping with rage. Hatred is boiling through my blood and my breathing is heavy almost like a hiss.

HEARING THEM TALK ABOUT THIS, I AM NOW CERTAIN that these assholes are responsible for the death of the only woman that I've loved. Not in a romantic sense, but the person who meant the world to my family. The one person I wasn't able to protect.

MY EYES WATER WITH THIS REVELATION. I RUN MY HANDS through my freshly washed hair, gripping at the scalp and pulling. I've got to get my shit together. I can't fuck this up.

I CAN PICTURE THE LAST TIME WE SPOKE, WHICH WAS over a year ago.

"I WANT TO BRING HOME JACE TO MEET EVERYBODY," SHE whispers. She's good, she knows if she gets through me, everyone else will follow.

"THAT FUCKER AIN'T NO GOOD FOR YOU. YOU KNOW THEY'LL rip him apart, right? What is he, an accountant?"

. . .

"MAXIM, KNOCK IT OFF. I'M IN LOVE WITH HIM," SHE *sniffles, making me feel like a jerk.*

KIND OF SUCKS FOR HER BEING IN A FAMILY WITH psychopaths. "I'll see what I can do," this is going to be a pain in the ass. "You know how dad is, everything stays in the family. This Jace guy of yours has nothing to do with the family, no connections, nothing."

I CAN PRACTICALLY HEAR HER SMILE THROUGH THE PHONE. "Thank you," her voice is louder and happier. "I'll see you guys later, I love you." I don't say anything back, I just disconnect the call.

THINKING BACK ON THAT MOMENT, I WISH I WOULD have said something back. I wish I would have told her to run, to hide, that I'm coming for her.

JAX AND ANNA'S VOICES START TO PLAY THROUGH THE speakers in the lonely room. Since I destroyed the headset and the cable attached to it, their voices flood everywhere.

. . .

THE RAGE IN ME IS SIMMERING DOWN LISTENING TO HER sweet voice and reminding me of what really matters. It's time now that I get ready for tonight, see you soon Anna.

CHAPTER 7

*a*nna

What exactly does someone wear to dinner, when they've never had a man cook for them at their house before? After staring at my closet for twenty minutes straight, I decided to do me. What I would feel the most comfortable in.

I did find myself reaching for my cargo pants, but even I have a little more class than that. Instead, I opted for a pair of tight jeans, a green silk blouse and thick wool socks. The only shoes I have with me are my cargo boots.

The phone brings me out of my stupor. I feel like I'm back in high school again trying to get ready for my first date. I groan as I answer the phone.

"Hello," I really should have looked at who is calling.

"Hey, how are you feeling today?" Jax's eerily calm voice comes through the line.

"I'm doing pretty good, how are you?" I wonder exactly why he's calling. He wouldn't call just to check up on me, he would send a text or have Colt call me.

"I'm fine, listen, we landed another big job. This one is one of the biggest ones that we've had, and it happens to deal with the chief of staff for the president. He believes that his daughter's been taken. There's not much information on it yet but that's what we're hoping to find out. I'm actually pulling in Mason in for this job."

He became quiet most likely waiting to see if I have a reaction or getting his thoughts together.

"So, does this mean that you need me to take on the senator case?" I'm nervous and excited at the same time, this will be the first job I've done in over three months.

"Yes, I do. Do you think you're up for it?"

"Explain everything to me, then I'll let you know, and is this a solo one or will I have a partner?"

"The boy is four-year-old, Johnny Sinclair and his father's name is Patrick...."

I interrupt him before he can finish, "I heard that story on the radio, it just happened a couple of days ago. The non-custodial father took him."

"That sounds like it. We received an anonymous tip from one of the staff members of the senator on how they heard him talking about a purchase he just made. Apparently, the staff member was eavesdropping and started hearing more details about the child. Where to put him, food and etc. And that arrangements would be made for him in the basement. No staff is allowed down there."

I can hear Jax take a deep breath, I know this case is bothering him before he continues. "Our first priority is bringing this kid home safely, then the cops and FBI are going to raid his house to see what else might be in the basement. To answer your earlier question, you will be doing this job by yourself. I know you like to work alone. But, we are going to have a couple of men close by in case there's another problem, which there shouldn't be. Anna, that was one tiny fluke. Don't let the past bother you from who you are and how good you are at your job."

My eyes burn from unshed tears. I know the Sophie case will always haunt me. She's the one innocent victim that I couldn't save. But, I also know that I need to try for this boy. No one expects a woman to show up to rescue him I'm more of a distraction, a deadly distraction.

I take in a deep breath, realizing I already know what I'm going to do, "I'll do it."

"I knew you would, it will be fine. I'll text you all the information and I want you to start surveillance, probably tomorrow for the next several days. This case is a little different, since this boy is so young, we don't want him in the Senators care for that long. In all honesty, we don't have any proof of what the Senator will do."

"Okay, send it to me right away so I can get started I got a few hours to work on it." I do already have my clothes picked out for tonight and the house is spotless. Plus, Maxim is bringing dinner. This is actually a welcome distraction, if I had more time, I would actually run over and try to do some spot surveillance now.

I decide to dig into as much research as I can, so I grab my notebook, laptop, my favorite pen and my cell phone, which is already sitting on the dining room table.

I make a fresh pot of coffee and grab a water bottle and a Gatorade. I'm a little weird but I like to have multiple drinks and I like to be thoroughly set up.

With coffee in hand, I start looking through articles on the laptop of all the information I find about little Johnny and Patrick. I even research his mom and other family members. Even though they say Patrick took him, another member might be involved behind the scenes.

With the *M.E.T.* connections, I have access to different databases and information that we might need, that the normal person couldn't get access to unless they have a warrant or special permission. Plus, if I need help Mason's fiancée, Lee, is a whiz at research and information gathering.

I check out arrest records on all family members. Patrick's is the only one that has turned up a little shady, mostly drug possession, small-time. The fraternal and maternal side of the family comes up clean.

I make an Excel spreadsheet and use my notebook to take notes. This way I can find out information fast, including repetitive actions for Patrick. Does Johnny need anything special, is he allergic to anything? That makes me snap my fingers since he's a child. I would like to stop and get him a stuffed animal, maybe a dinosaur. This boy isn't going to trust me, I'm a stranger no matter how nice I seem.

Decked out in all my gear with a knife attached to my leg, doesn't make me look sweet and welcoming to a small child.

Glancing at the clock while printing off my spreadsheet I realize I only got a freaking half an hour to get ready.

In rush mode, I was able to get everything cleaned up. I got dressed in my previously picked outfit and adding just a slight touch of makeup to my face, I hate that shit, I am ready.

I still have five minutes to spare, but of course, there is a knock at the door, and Maxim is early.

I quickly check myself in the mirror by the door and knock on the wooden table that my dad made for good luck.

Opening the door, Maxim gives me his best smile, he looks so intense.

Three bags of groceries are on his arm. The same arm is holding a bottle of champagne, and his other hand, his injured one, has a beautiful selection of roses. At first, they make me cringe because I think about my stupid stalker, he loves to send roses. As I look closer I can tell they're the kind that are made with different colors, they're beautiful, purple, red, pink and even a dab of orange in the middle.

"Do you want to let me in or are you just going to stand there and stare at me?" Maxim winks.

"Oh, I'm sorry, come right in." Embarrassment flows through me, my face lightly turning my cheeks a shade of pink like the roses.

Maxim walks into the kitchen, he knows where it is since he was here earlier. I shiver, remembering how bad his hand looked I glance down, and he's got a small bandage on both sides. It must have healed pretty well.

His jeans tightly hug his ass giving me a drool-worthy view as he walks to the kitchen. I want to say how he swaggers but it's not that, it's just him representing himself with confidence.

Maxim sets the stuff down on the counter as I follow behind and look for a vase to put the roses in. As soon as I cut the stems and put them in the water, my arm is grabbed, and I'm swirled around.

I yelp as Maxim grabs me under the arms and lifts me up onto the counter next to the flowers. He positions himself in between my legs as he moves a piece of hair behind my ears.

"All I've been thinking about is doing this, I can't get your mouth off my mind." He looks between my eyes and my mouth. I have a sudden urge to lick my bottom lip, but I don't want to seem like it was planned, so instead, I just bite it which seems ten times worse.

He runs his hands up and down my thighs, making heat travel straight to my core. I grab his shoulders and pull him closer to me I need the friction and I need his touch, but more than anything, I need his mouth on me.

Getting the hint, he grabs me by the back of the neck and his other hand reaches around my back pulling me closer, at the same time he lightly presses his lips to mine.

I need more right away. I pull him harder towards me and try to make the kiss heavier. Maxim chuckles then wraps his hand in my hair forcing my face back just an inch.

"God, you are so beautiful and responsive." I just stare back into those beautiful blue eyes.

Maxim quickly grabs my hip with both hands, brings me to the edge, and presses his glorious body right against me.

I can feel how hard and big he is. How much he wants me but there's so much clothing in between us, *why are we wearing clothes?*

His lips slam down onto mine, forcing my mouth open with his tongue, he frantically but expertly tastes and explorers everything that is me, as I do the same to him.

I can't get enough of this freaking guy.

I lift his shirt and start to push my hands up, wanting to feel his ripped skin, when he grabs both of my wrists pulling away from me.

"Damn girl," he laughs. "I promised I'd feed you and that's what my intentions are, but later I'll take care of you." Maxim wipes off the remnants of our kiss with his thumb and lifts me off the counter.

God that was hot!

CHAPTER 8

*a*nna

"So, what are we having for dinner?" I sit on a bar stool at the island and watch him cook.

"I wasn't sure exactly what you like. Since you got some Italian blood in you, I figured we'd go that way." He turns around and looks at me. "I want to make you my mother's Russian lasagna."

I laugh I've never heard of anything like that. "Is that an actual thing?"

"Oh yeah, just because I'm Russian, doesn't mean that my family doesn't enjoy good Italian food. We just like to use a lot more sausage and different cheeses and our sauce is homemade. I remember the women at home using lard, but I don't do that."

I groan, very happy with that, it would stick right on my ass. We idly chat while Maxim works on dinner. Once he puts it into the oven he pours us both a glass of champagne and then motions me over to the couch. I sit right next to him, wanting to be close.

I realize I'm sitting next to this man and I don't even know that much about him. I put my glass on the coffee table and lean back grabbing his hand, holding it in mine.

"Tell me about yourself. Besides you being my neighbor, I've only known you for two days." He squeezes my hand and then put his glass on the coffee table.

Turning his body so he's facing me, he asks. "What is it you'd like to know?"

"Really anything you think of, even the stupid stuff, like your favorite color. How about we take turns telling the other person something about us?"

"Okay, that sounds good. I'll start I'm originally from New York." I laugh hearing that, I already knew this.

Maybe if I'm more personal, he will be, "I have four older brothers, and I've lived a pretty sheltered existence."

Maxim winces a little bit like this bothered him, very strange. "I have one brother and two sisters. I'm the oldest." Very straightforward, absolutely no emotion.

"What made you decide to buy a cabin here?"

"I just needed to get away from New York, the hustle and bustle of it all." He states as he reaches for his champagne glass.

"Yeah, me, too, it's really quiet here and the fresh air is wonderful. So, what do you do for a living?" I smile at him.

"I actually dabble in a few things. I have several small businesses that I own but construction is the main one." Maxim takes a drink then sets down his glass. "What do you do for a living?"

"I work in my family business. I guess my job title would mainly be a researcher." This is the same thing I tell everybody when they ask me what I do for a living. "What is your last name?"

He was quiet for a few seconds, then the oven went off for the lasagna. Maybe he doesn't want to tell me? He quickly got up and went over to the oven, taking it out to cool off for a few minutes while he threw together a salad. I grab both of our glasses and walk over to where he's at sitting down at the island just to watch him. I don't think I've ever seen a more magnificent looking man, between his chiseled features and the way he holds himself.

I find my thoughts drifting and I realize that I really want to see his ass. I bet it's even better looking naked than it is in those jeans. I'll settle just seeing him in a tight pair of boxers.

Yeah, that would make me seem kind of weird if I just asked him to pull his pants down. Fuck it, he can just take off his jeans while he finishes cooking. I smile knowingly to myself.

"What are you smiling for? Are you ogling me

again? I'm starting to feel like a piece of meat. It's making me very uncomfortable." My mouth opens as he busts out laughing. I should have known better. I still have yet to meet that one man who doesn't like attention.

We sit down to eat. He is an unbelievable cook. "This is freaking amazing!"

"Thank you, my mom's been making this for us since we were kids. Ever since her and my dad visited Italy they just love the food and the culture." We sit in silence for a few minutes just enjoying the food and the company, then I realized I want to spend a lot more time with this man. I want him in my life and in my bed, but I am going to be gone several days to several weeks.

"I start a new job tomorrow," I blurt out.

His fork full of food stops halfway up to his mouth, "oh, really? Are you excited?" Maxim finishes the food and puts his fork down, facing my way.

"Actually, very excited a little bit nervous, too, but I haven't worked in several months and I really want to get back to it." He just studies me for several seconds gauging my reaction. I can't really figure this man out.

"So exactly what will you be doing?" Maxim rests his hand on the back of my barstool massaging my shoulder with his thumb.

My family has always warned me about revealing too much information. This can mean the loss of friendships and relationships, and plus you never know who's listening. We definitely don't want the information in the wrong hands. I do trust Maxim but I'm only going to give a little bit, at least until I know he's not going to run scared of a woman that could probably kick his ass.

"I'm actually going to be working on a research case. It's for a kidnapping victim, a young boy. My family has helped a lot of other families find missing people." I stop talking and just let that settle for a minute, watching his expression. His eyes and body are stone cold, no emotion.

"Are you guys like private detectives. You do this better than the police?" It might seem like a rude question, but it's not, we get this a lot.

"We have a lot more connections and a lot more money than the police do. Plus, more drive to help innocent victims. My family has been doing this for decades. I guess you could call us private detectives to a certain extent. I don't think my brothers would like that though." I smile thinking of the glares and disgusting comments I would get if my called my brothers' private dicks. "We are more focused on the victim side in the family and we are good at finding people that are in high-risk situations."

"That sounds pretty cool. I would imagine this can be scary sometimes. Is it ever dangerous, has anyone tried to ever hurt you?"

This is where the questions get too intense and can go in another direction. At this point, I always try to refocus the conversation. I shake my head in a small gesture hoping he'll leave it at that, and I decide to ask a heavier question. I'm a woman, what do you expect. "So, what is this thing between us, and are you seeing anyone now?"

I am curious about his answer, even though I threw him for a loop. Shock briefly flashes in his eyes before he was able to recover.

"No, I'm not seeing anyone. All I want to do is spend my time with you."

I shake my head no again and bite my lip. I'm getting butterflies and glorious tingles all over. Maxim lifts me up and I immediately straddle him. Damn, this boy is hard already. Does that thing ever go down?

"I've wanted you since the first time I saw you, Anna. I can't stop thinking about you, I can't get enough of you." As he talks, he slowly trails kisses down the side of my neck and behind my ear.

I groan and lean my head back to give him better access. His hands come up cupping my breasts while his thumbs tweak my nipples. This instinctively makes me start circling my hips, hoping to get a lot more friction, my body has a mind of its own.

He pulls my hips down hard on him hitting me at my core. As his mouth finds mine, we wrestle with our tongues for control for several minutes. His magnificent fingers explore my body under my shirt and bra.

My shirt is ripped over my head and my bra disappears before I even realize it. I feel a little embarrassed being naked from the waist up, but I'm so turned on right now, I don't even care.

"Stand up," Maxim demands, his voice husky.

I instantly obey. Maxim starts to work my tight jeans down over my thighs and helps me step out of them. Standing up next to me he lowers me down on the couch.

Spreading my knees with his hands, he leans down and inhales, his voice turning to a hungry growl. Maxim's arm moves up to cup my breast, while he lightly uses his fingers to trace the outside of my panties.

I'm fascinated by watching him, I want to close my eyes and put my head back to enjoy it. This man is so mesmerizing.

His finger slips in the side of my silky black panties and immediately finds my core pushing all the way in. I clench instantly and throw my head back. He starts to work his magical finger in and out fast. His thumb agonizingly plays with my clit.

I hear him growl again as his hand disappears. I want to cry out and tell him not to stop, but when I look down, he has my panties in both hands ripping them apart, throwing them to the side.

"God, you smell so fucking good, like innocence that I want to destroy."

My thighs are pushed open as wide as they can go. His thick thumbs hold open my pussy lips while he licks from the bottom to the top and then focuses on my clit.

Two fingers are pushed in hard and start pumping to a beat that's only playing in his head. I thought it would be too much, but it feels so damn good, his mouth sucks, flicks and teases my clit.

It doesn't take me more than a few minutes before I start screaming out his name. When I come down, he slows down his movements, making sure to lick my orgasm away.

Holy shit, I thought the other night was hot, this blew everything out of the water like a freaking Fourth of July explosion.

"Are you okay?" Maxim asks, lifting me up and wrapping a blanket around me.

"Oh God yes", I blurt out. "Wait, what about you?" I ask him as he comes back from grabbing us both a bottle of water.

"This was about you. I don't want to go too fast, but you really looked like you needed a release." He smirks, winking at me.

"I don't mind," I tell him, but it sounds more like I'm begging. Shit, maybe we should slow down till I have the courage to tell him I'm a virgin.

Maxim wraps his arms around me, "I want to see you again real soon. I imagine you'll be busy with your job but whenever you get a minute, let me know."

Nodding my head, I feel really sleepy, it must be the orgasmic bliss. Maxim kisses me on the forehead, his knuckles graze over my cheek as he whispers 'goodbye' then leaves.

The smile doesn't leave my face as I put away the leftovers in the kitchen. I'll clean up the rest tomorrow. I didn't even bother getting dressed. I need to get some rest. I start another job tomorrow.

I imagine I'll sleep all night with a smile on my face.

CHAPTER 9

*a*nna

This day went nothing like I would've expected it to. Granted, the weather was still beautiful for January in the Colorado mountains. It made the thirty-minute drive to Aspen enjoyable. I've always loved the scenery up here, even during a blizzard. Nothing could ever beat the natural beauty of nature and the mountains.

OF COURSE, ME BEING ME, ALWAYS LETS THE GAS GAUGE run to almost empty for some reason. Maybe it's just a thrill I get for thinking I'm living dangerously. Stranded on the side of the road with no heat or food during a blizzard. Or, I happen to be picked up by the most elusive serial killer in North America.

Either scenario I need gas, and thankfully I made it into Aspen just in time.

After I finish pumping, I notice an older model car pull in on the side of the convenience store. A man and a younger boy get out.

My breath catches when I get a good look at the little boy. He looks a lot like Johnny. But, the man with him is not the Senator-it must be his father.

Quickly walking over there, I don't hesitate at all, I stop next to the boy facing the father. The boy's face is dirty, and his tear stained eyes are severely puffy. This isn't the type of face that looks like he's in trouble from a loving parent. It's the type that emits deep sadness, it's the type that is terrified and scared to death.

I step in between the two of them as the father shuts the backdoor where the boy was, my back facing the man. He's a decent size build, with a bit of a paunch. Several of his teeth are missing and his face is pockmarked. He's just as dirty if not more so than the boy is. Did they stay in the car for the last several days?

In twenty years of training, this is the one thing that would have my ass kicked by my trainers, brothers and father. Never turn your back to an opponent or someone that can seriously hurt you.

I started training when I was two years old. My brothers also started around the same age.

In the beginning, it was basically just karate. Then I would move on to harder things as I got older, like taekwondo, Jujitsu, Aikido and my favorite, Krav

Maga. I would continue to do everything while training in different areas.

Our schedule was grueling a few hours every day with only Sundays off, plus we still went to school and had our normal lives. When we turned thirteen our father put us in kickboxing. He wanted us to learn more local and street fighting.

Since we started early all of us excelled and we love it. Each of us took on our own identities, as I use knives. Colt uses his fists. Finn uses his knowledge of the body and medicine. Mason uses guns. Jax uses everything, whatever is available. He is still the deadliest of us all.

When my father's sister was twenty-six years old, she was murdered by her husband. Her kids had to watch. It tore my father, grandparents and his siblings apart.

He and his brothers thought of MET *Moretti Extraction Team*. They never could've imagined how big it would get.

My aunt that was murdered, her children, my cousins, are a huge part of the team. None of them want to be in charge, they just like the field work and helping to save innocents like their mother.

My thoughts return to the present. I don't want the little guy to see his father when I ask him a question. "Sweetie, is your name Johnny Sinclair?"

"Yes, ma'am." Johnny whispers as hiccups take over, most likely from crying so much.

I can hear the deep breathing behind me and the slam of a fist on the car's roof. The noise makes both of us jump. I remember the radio announcer and my research saying this guy was armed and dangerous. I can't let this boy go anywhere with him anymore. This case, I'm intervening early.

Even though I might've got myself into more shit than I can handle.

Facing the disgusting excuse for a human being, I fist my hands at my side and spread my legs slightly into a fighting stance.

"Johnny, come here," the guy growls, looking around me talking to his son.

Stepping back slightly, I grab the boy's hand, making sure he knows to stay. "He's not going anywhere with you. He's going to be going home with his mom as soon as the police get here."

"You need to move the fuck out of the way bitch," he yells, as spit flies from his mouth landing on the cement ground between us. His whole demeanor has changed. Patrick went from in control to angry.

Moving around me, he grabs his son by the arm, jerking the boy towards him. At the same time, he opens the car door and starts to shove Johnny inside.

I can't let this happen, I won't let this happen. Dread fills me knowing that if this man gets away, what he could possibly do to him. I don't want to sit there and play tug-of-war with the boy between us.

"Sir, the police are looking for you. This boy is not

in your custody, you can't take him. Look at him, he's scared." I try being nice. Maybe he'll listen to reason and see that this whole situation is absurd. "Do you really want to go to jail?"

Patrick pauses for a minute. "Lady, there will be no heroes today. This is my son and I have every right to take him." He pushes harder on the boy wanting him to get in the car faster. Johnny smacks his head against the side of the door due to Patrick's bad maneuvering. He silently cries not wanting to further piss off his father.

I sigh, closing my eyes and letting my head drop down. This is not a situation I wanted to be in. Don't get me wrong, I'm sure as shit not letting the strange man take this boy. I was just hoping to not have to use force. I at least wanted to stick to the words that Jax told me before I left New York.

Stay out of trouble, and absolutely no fighting. Nobody needs a dead hero.

The irate child abuser moves back from the door getting ready to shut it after Johnny is secured inside. I push him back with enough force that gives me time to carefully remove Johnny from the car.

"Hey buddy, run inside and tell them to call 911." I say with authority pointing over at the entrance to the store.

Johnny takes off in a run just as Patrick regains his balance. "You fucking bitch. I told you to leave this alone." He growls almost silently. I can tell his anger has multiplied to a dangerous level. He starts to reach into his coat pocket. I can see the end of the gun as he pulls it out fast, without warning.

I'm in my zone, this is what I've been trained for. I'm aware of my surroundings and what I need to do. I'm in survival mode.

Ready, I can feel the anger and worry abate. My fist flies through the air, hitting Patrick right in the throat. I don't do it too hard or too soft. I don't want to crush his trachea, killing the bastard, he needs to be alive. He deserves to do time, prisoners don't like when people hurt their kids. Especially since most of them haven't seen their own in years.

Patrick instantly clutches his throat and starts to gasp for air. Right now, he'll be able to get small amounts, limited but enough to survive.

I reach into his car grabbing the phone charger I saw when he was trying to push Johnny back in. Kicking the back of his knee. I want him to sit down on the ground, which he does immediately. He has no fight left in him, which is good. Making use of the charger cord, I tie his hands tightly behind his back.

He'll need to wait here for several minutes, at least until he fully regains control of his breathing.

I walk over to bystanders watching us in the front of the store, keeping an eye on Patrick. I don't want the boy anywhere near his father.

"Did you call the police?" An employee in uniform turns in my direction, then nods yes.

I pull Johnny to me and wrap him in a warm hug. Chills spread throughout making me slightly shake. It's just an adrenaline rush, I taper it down, trying to sooth the little guy. He's shaking more than I am.

We pull apart as we hear the sirens. Multiple police, fire and ambulances are driving down Main Street. Well, that's a lot, they must have had help from multiple towns, every man and woman on the force.

Johnny keeps stealing glances at his father on the ground. It looks like he's waiting for him to jump up and grab him. I bend down to his level and rub his arms. "He can't hurt you anymore, the police are almost here, and they will call your mom." Johnny smiles, which melts my heart. His beautiful brown eyes pool with tears, making them glisten. I can see the change in the little man as his cheeks pink with excitement.

Thirty minutes later, we are surrounded by the whole Aspen, Mountainside and surrounding towns police force. There are two ambulances and several fire trucks. The fire trucks are the older style. I can't keep my eyes off of them, they just look so cool and antique.

A woman of average height, fairly pretty but not model status, jumps out of the police car and runs straight towards Johnny. I smile, this must be his mother.

She hugs his little body so tight that I can hear him groan. I sat next to the little guy for the past thirty minutes in the back of a squad car with a cop right outside the door. As soon as Johnny saw his mom coming, he jumped out of the car.

My hand is grabbed, and I'm being pulled out of the car door by a woman with the same eyes as Johnny. I didn't even hear her open the door.

"T-thank you, thank you so m-much," I can barely make out what she says through her hysterical sobbing. She clinches to me hard, like she can't hug me tight enough. I wrap my arms around her returning the favor, letting my hand go up and down her back in a soothing motion.

"What you did is beyond words," she's calmed down some. "You saved my son. Thank you so much." She releases me to hold tightly to my hand.

"I just happened to be in the right place at the right time." Johnny comes over and stands next to her. She releases my hand and lifts him into another hug, smothering his face with elated kisses.

"My name is Monica, and you obviously met Johnny."

"My name is Anna," I hold out my hand and she shakes it. Looking at Johnny, "we haven't been properly introduced," I move my hand over to him and he shakes it, giggling the whole time. It's wonderful to hear him laughing after what he just went through.

Monica gives us both the teary smile, "please, have dinner with us. It's the least I could do. I've seen you around Mountainside, that's where we live."

"That would be great, I would love to," and I meant

it. It would be good for me to make some friends that are not family or business associates.

Monica chats with me for several more minutes. She and Johnny are real sweethearts. We decide on dinner next week, she figured it would be best to give Johnny time to rest.

Patrick was hauled out of here almost immediately. The police quickly lifted him up into a standing position and slammed him against the back of the car, replacing the phone charger with cuffs. He just growled and cursed the whole time. He never looked at Johnny.

CHAPTER 10

*M*axim

I've got to say, curiosity is the reason I'm driving to Aspen in this rented white Dodge Ram. I had one of the men go grab this for me, it's the best way for me to keep from being noticed.

My guys are following behind, maintaining their positions of being unnoticed.

Anna piqued my interest yesterday when she said she was going out on another job after being gone for several months. I would like to know exactly how her family operates.

I don't believe for one minute or even one second that the Moretti's are good people. Soon they will realize they never should have fucked with us.

It took almost the rest of the night when I got home to figure out what this new job was. I had every contact

I could think of running through databases and even reaching out to their personal contacts.

We finally got a hit when someone mentioned they overheard a conversation between a Senator and some other guy, of course, this is the staff. People should know better, especially people with money to ever trust their staff.

They will be the first ones to sell you out in a heartbeat, well besides family members, in my experience. I have several very loyal employees that have been with me for years, but I still keep things to myself.

Apparently, the Moretti's got wind of this job and their main contact person is the maternal grandparents. I don't even think that the mother knows where the child is or what the father was planning on doing.

I've been curious about Anna's role is in all of this. I know she says that she's the researcher but being part of the original siblings, I think she would have more responsibility than just sitting at a computer all day and checking Facebook and other social media sites.

She looks like nothing, anyone could take her on. I don't believe she's had any training, well maybe some basic self-defense, but I can't imagine anything else past that.

She's someone I would enjoy to take my time breaking. I smile as I reach the turnoff for the Aspen exit. The weather is quite wonderful, it's making for a pleasant day.

It would be better if it was cloudy and maybe even

snowing. I have a vehicle that doesn't really stand out, but I still don't want to be noticed.

The GPS is programmed in the truck. I make my way through Aspen to the Senator's house. My thoughts keep going back to Anna from last night and how good she tasted, smelled and how she was so fucking responsive. Most of the women I've been with just fake it.

I know I'm not done with her, yet. I haven't gotten my fill. I think I'll start with the oldest brother and work my way down through the family, saving the delectable Anna for last.

The brothers won't be that easy to get, all of them are exceptionally trained. Even though I have more men and more money, I don't want to take any chances of being found out.

I will start to pick them off one by one and that should give me plenty of time to do everything I want to my neighbor.

It won't be long before I take her, and unbeknownst to her, she's going to be giving me a lot of information that's useful in targeting her brothers.

My eyes roll as I pull across the street to get a good glimpse of the Senators mansion.

The Senator comes from old money and new money. No other Senator could afford a place like this. It takes up at least four blocks in the center of Aspen. It just seems like a waste of space.

More money, comes more power, even I should know that, but this is ridiculous.

The house is an older Victorian with guards leisurely walking around. I was only able to spot four, but I imagine that there have to be several inside.

My interest is definitely piqued. I want to see how Anna does this job. Will she be able to get into the house? Will she do it by sneaking in or being invited in?

I start to laugh a little now. I bet you that woman has some fire I don't even know about.

I pull out my phone and call my right-hand guy, Booker. It's a nickname that sneaky bastard has. None of us really know how he got it.

"What's up boss?" He answers on the second ring.

"Not much, just wanted to see if you found anything out about the Moretti's locations, where they are now and the most important, job information."

"We know where Jax and Colt are, but Mason and Finn are harder to track down, their jobs differentiate almost every day. And I'm sure you know where that sweet ass of a baby sister is," Booker gloats.

My hands are flexing at my side, this shouldn't even piss me off, but it does. I feel like I have ownership of this girl, protective instinct and that makes me very mad. It's useless to own something that you're going to kill.

"Anna Moretti was just assigned a new job, it's the one I had you look into, Johnny Sinclair. Anyway, I'm at the Senator's house right now doing a stakeout just to see if I can get any information to see how she handles these cases."

"Boss, you don't need to do that. That's what we're here for. I can have a couple of guys there within the half hour with surveillance equipment and they can videotape the whole damn thing." He explains sounding annoyed.

"No, this is something I need to see for myself, I'll be fine. I've got guys with me. I'll keep you updated if I need anything else, just make sure you keep working on finding the location for the other two brothers. I'll take care of the neighbor. I think I'm going to use her to get some information on the missing pieces of the puzzle.

Booker laughs, "well, that should be fun and keep you entertained for a while."

I hang up the phone, no reason for niceties, good-bye is good-bye. I start scanning the neighborhood to see if anybody is watching me or watching the Senator's house.

No movement, nothing has happened for over forty-five minutes. That's the time when I hear the sirens.

The front door to the Victorian house opens up as two men come racing out like the damn things on fire. I recognize one of the men as the senator, the other one must be a bodyguard.

The guard quickly usher's the Senator into the back

of a Land Rover and runs around to the driver's seat. The car starts immediately and takes off going in the opposite direction that the police cars are coming from.

I move down the street just a little bit I don't want to be caught too close to the Senator's house since I'm not sure what this is about. Several cop cars with sirens blaring and several unmarked cars slam on their brakes right in front of the Senators house.

I can tell the unmarked cars are FBI, signaling my time to go.

Where the hell is Anna? I called my guys that were following me and told them to figure out what's going on.

The drive back to Mountainside seemed to take half the time as the drive to Aspen. I can't get my thoughts off what happened. Was she able to get in and out without me noticing? Is this woman that good?

I know I'll find out later. I planned on sending her a text message anyway, from the way she made it sound she was going to stay in Aspen for a little while.

When I pull into my driveway, I notice Gina's little red sports car with her in it. A flash of irritation goes through me. I laugh a little bit, it would be hilarious if a blizzard happens right now. I'd send her to the only available hotel in Mountainside, maybe even makė her ass walk there.

A text alert refocuses my attention. Apparently, the job was finished earlier. The cops were eager to share the news with everyone, including my guys. Damn, Anna got lucky. I really wanted to see her in action.

I grab my stuff out of the truck and start to walk by her towards the front door, I know she'll follow me. I really don't have time for idle chitchat. Sometimes Gina can be a pain in the ass to get rid of. I can see my men making themselves invisible in case Anna returns home.

After dropping my stuff off in my office, I come back in the living room and Gina is stark naked with red high heels on. She's slowly running her fingertips over the couch, in a sultry way.

I can't say that my dick got hard for her because it's been hard ever since I met Anna. But damn, I could sure use a release right now.

I slowly start to walk towards her and undo the buttons of my shirt.

"Did you miss me, baby?" She purrs as she runs her hands up and down her body.

"No, bend over the couch." She does exactly what I say as I push my jeans and boxers down to my ankles. No reason to get undressed, she won't be staying long.

CHAPTER 11

*a*nna
    Johnny and his mother had left about half an hour earlier. I was asked a while ago to give a statement to the FBI and the state police. Who knows when that will be?

There's nothing better to do to pass my time then people watch. I would like to give Jax a call and explain the situation, but as soon as I pick up my phone, that's when they're going to want to talk, so I'll wait till everything is done.

The cops are all running around frantically looking for any more evidence. It looks as though Patrick Sinclair's car has been ripped apart by forensics and CSI. One would think they would take that to a shop and do it there. Not these guys. I think they want this case done and over with, closed.

There was probably over thirty cops here that

included personnel and FBI, but now there only seems to be about five remaining.

"Ma'am, would you mind following us so we can take your statement?" I whip my head around from my people watching. I didn't even hear them come up. One guy is overweight and older than me in a police uniform, he's standing with another man in a well-tailored suit, looking ready for a date night, not an interview.

"That's totally fine, but please don't call me ma'am it's Anna." The officer stretches his hand for me to follow, he has a nice and friendly smile. The other man has a stone-cold expression, he reminds me of Maxim, just not as good looking.

They both lead me to a little cafe down the block. I'm incredibly relieved that we are not going to the police station. I don't do very good in interrogation rooms, even as a witness or an informant. It creeps me out and gets on my nerves.

We spend the next hour and a half going over the events of the day, starting with my research last night, to my needing gas this morning.

They both nod in agreement when I said I just got a lucky break that I didn't have to stake out the Senators house.

Besides the *M.E.T.* I was asked to keep this case on the down-low, since it is high-profile, they want to make sure that it's handled right.

Both men walk me back to my car and I start

driving back to Mountainside. I decide to put the phone on speaker, this is the best time to talk to Jax.

I want to get this over with, so when I get back, I can see Maxim. That man has been on my mind all freaking day. I would love to take things to the next level for us, and that definitely means sex. At first, I thought I would never be ready, but I am oh so ready now.

My nipples harden and butterflies swarm low in my belly just thinking about it.

Jax picks up on the third ring, he might have been busy. "What's up?"

"Just wanted to give you a heads up. I went to start the surveillance job today and drove to Aspen. You know how I always like to let my gas tank run empty, so I pulled over and got gas. Guess who was at the gas station?" I smile waiting for his reply. I'm either going to get yelled at or he's going to be impressed.

"Who was it Anna, I'm ready to go into a meeting, and I don't have the time right now." He snaps.

Wow, crabby much. "It was Johnny and Patrick Sinclair."

"What? What did you do? Why didn't you call us? I told you I would have guys on standby for this." I can hear how mad he is, his voice is very clipped.

"Honestly, I didn't even think about it. My only focus was saving this child. He was really bad looking, Jax and terrified. I wasn't going to have another Sofia incident, I had to act fast. They were just stopping at the store, they were going to be in and out." I take a deep breath as the tears burn my eyes, my heart hurts for that little guy.

"Okay, I'm sorry I snapped at you. I understand, but damn girl, with everything that's happened to you, I can't lose my sister, my only sister." His voice skips as the emotion comes through his words. I actually feel a little guilty now.

"I love you, too, big brother." I tell him with as much sincerity as I can. I love all my brother's to death. I would die for them.

I tell Jax everything that happened, starting from when I realized I was pretty much out of gas, and up until the time I called him.

We said our goodbyes when I reach the cabin. I know he's relieved that I'm fine and that the case is closed.

Pulling up in the two-car driveway, two things I notice almost immediately. The first one is that Maxim has company, there's a red sports car over there. Who the hell drives a sports car, in the mountains, in the winter?

I'll just have to ask him. I would like to change and wash this day away from me before I go over and see him. Maybe one of his sisters is visiting him. That would be really cool to meet some of his family.

The second thing is the package that's on my doorstep. I did not order anything. Dread slowly fills up and takes over every living cell in my body, making me feel sick. This has to be from my stalker.

I take a deep breath, then slowly get out of my car, grabbing my things. I wish I could just bypass the front door and go through the back, pretending this package never existed, but I know I can't.

Getting to the front door, I unlock it and purposely step over the box. It looks like it's about the size of a brand-new pair of shoes. If the guy really knew me, he would send me a new pair of combat boots, mine are starting to get worn.

I involuntary shiver, that's horrible to think, maybe it's a she. If they realize I accepted one of their gifts, then I'll never see the end of it.

I go and unload all my stuff from the day, even my overnight bag since I won't be needing it, the jobs done. Time to get this over with.

The gift is wrapped in expensive pink paper with a beautiful white lace bow. Inside on the top above the tissue paper is a note. I take another deep breath and open it.

I want you to wear this
on our first night together

Of course, that will never happen in a freaking million years. This guy went beyond knight in shining armor to creep mode.

I remove the tissue from the box, gently placing the card to the side, trying not to touch that much of the surface in case it can be fingerprinted later.

There's some of the skimpiest white lingerie I have ever seen. I gag a little bit. My sanity and safety seem to be at risk, and this does not make me feel good. I may be able to fight but you never know whom you're going up against. Are they better than you? Are they deadlier or sneakier?

It's getting close to the point where I'm going to have to tell my brothers. I take out my phone and take a picture of the offending item, then send it to the printer in the office so I can attach it to the card.

I grab the box with one hand, trying not to touch it more than needed and take it into the garage, throwing it in the trash bin. I'm not going to let this get me down, now it's time for me to get ready. I have to go see a gorgeous hot neighbor.

I shower quickly, which is a miracle for me and decide on comfortable clothes. Almost the same stuff that I met Maxim in at the grocery store. A pair of black leggings, my boots (because I still don't have another pair of shoes) and a really thick sweater with a light t-shirt underneath.

I pull my hair into a tight bun at the base of my neck and add a little powder and mascara to my face, plus my trusty Chapstick. I think it's cherry flavor so that should give me a little color.

I feel giddy like a schoolgirl, I practically skip over to Maxim's house.

My pulse is pounding as I lift my hand to knock on the front door, that's when I noticed that it's slightly open. Not enough for someone from the street to see but this close you can tell that the door wasn't closed.

The little hairs on my body rise up. Did someone break in? Is he okay?

I reach down to my inner thigh and silently curse myself, this time I didn't bring my knives. There's no time to go back so I push open the door.

"Hello," I call out, but obviously not loud enough to be overheard from the grunts and the moans.

I follow the direction of the noise. I'm in the small foyer right now and the living room is off to the right-hand side of the smaller Cottage.

I wish I would have just walked home. I wish I would have never talked to him again, but I didn't, my dumbass kept going in.

There is a naked woman bending over the back of a couch wearing high-heeled red stilettos. Her hair is blond and in great condition, she must use expensive products for it.

I can't see her face because Maxim has his hand pressed on the back of her head, pushing her into the sofa cushion.

Her ass is up in the air and Maxim is standing right behind her ramming hard into the back of her. *I finally have a view of his naked ass.* His jeans and boxers are down around his ankles. His other hand grips her hip as he keeps plowing into her.

Neither one of them realize that I'm here yet, but that changes the moment my mind comprehends what

I'm seeing. A loud gasp escapes me as the tears this time don't pool in my eyes, they run down my face.

Both of them look at me, the blonde Barbie is smirking while Maxim has a look of disgust on his face and maybe some of regret. He never stopped fucking her while he stared at me.

I don't stick around. With a broken heart and a crushed ego, let's not forget my trampled pride, I run back to my house. Locking the doors and setting the alarm, I grab a tub of chocolate ice cream from the freezer and decide I'm going to spend the next two days in bed.

Misery loves heartbroken company.

CHAPTER 12

*a*nna
　　The pounding in my head won't seem to abate, right now I'd give anything for this sucker to go away. I know I'm not hungover because I don't remember drinking. I groan inwardly, I'm probably getting some kind of flu.

I roll over on my side and instantly snuggle deeper into the silk sheets and the most comfortable bedspread I've ever used.

Instantly my eyes pop open and I sit up, regretting that move. My head pounds as I snap my eyes closed rubbing on my temples before I get a view of anything.

I don't own silk sheets, and the bedspread I'm using happens to be one that my mom made over twenty years ago, it's a very thick and heavy quilt.

After letting the throbbing subside, I slowly open my eyes, taking in my surroundings. I'm sitting in the middle of a four-poster bed that looks like it's made of intricate wood carvings. I might appreciate it if I knew where the hell I was.

The rest of the room is done in more of a nature design with browns and greens and a few yellow art pieces hanging up on the wall.

Three doors are in the room one to the left of me, and two straight in front of me. The whole right wall is covered with curtains, it must be one huge freaking window.

Where the hell am I? Why can't I remember what happened last night?

I'll contemplate that in a minute, my bladder feels like it's about ready to explode. I quickly jump off the bed onto the plush carpet, it feels really good on my bare feet. Looking down, I can recognize the outfit I have on, it's one of the many that I wear to bed. A pair of short gray shorts with a tight but not too tight tank top. No bra but at least I have on panties.

The door on the left is one of the biggest closets I've ever seen, empty. I finally find the bathroom straight ahead of me on the right. So that only leaves the left side to be the exit out of this mysterious place.

I'm a little bit curious about where I am but I'm not really nervous. I've been in so many weird situations that we are trained not to react until we know what's going on.

After relieving myself, I make my way out to explore my surroundings. Memories of last night start to creep up on me. I sit on the edge of the bed letting them flow through.

I remember being out cold in a deep sleep and hearing something like a smash of glass. Of course, I got up to investigate but thinking back, I wish I would've sent a message or let somebody know what I'm doing. Who really takes time to do that when they're investigating a strange noise in the house?

The cabin is freaking huge and I didn't grab any of my stuff, my knives or even my socks to keep my damn feet warm.

It was dark as I searched every room and every place. There was total silence, I couldn't find the glass or a disturbance anywhere.

Thinking about it now, it was just a gimmick to get me out of bed to investigate, and it worked.

The next thing I remember is a sharp pinch on the side of my neck and I woke up here. As I remembered the needle going into my neck, my hand reaches up to caress the swollen flesh. I wonder what they shot me up with?

No one would have drugged me if they expected me to come willingly, so that only means one thing, I was taken. Now I'm starting to get a little worried. We have multiple enemies everywhere.

Pacing the floor, I need a plan. The best thing that's always worked for me is to let them think that I'm still this weak breakable girl. Not many people know I'm highly trained, most girls my size and age aren't.

So, I will be a scared little girl. On instinct, not because I'm playing a part, I start to bite my fingernails still pacing when the left door, that I briefly tried to open before going to the bathroom, swings open with a big bang.

A gorgeous man with creamy cocoa skin stands in the entrance, his legs are spread apart prepared for anything and his hands are behind his back in a casual stance.

This guy is huge, muscles are growing on muscles everywhere. I've never seen anyone with dark silky-smooth skin that unblemished before. He does have a scar that goes through his left eyebrow and one on the side of his neck, but it still doesn't take away from his beauty. There's an aura of danger within him. This man can most likely kill me in two seconds flat, well it would be an interesting fight.

"Ms. Moretti, please follow me." I don't hesitate, I'm curious why the hell I'm here. I'm not going to bother asking, he doesn't look like the type to make friendly conversation.

We're at the end of a long hallway that has wooden stained trim and crown molding stretching the whole way. We've had to pass at least ten other doors, most likely leading to bathrooms, bedrooms or whatever rich people have. There are no personal pictures on the walls. I was really hoping to get a glimpse into who might be the owner. There's just more artwork splashed here, it's actually pretty good for abstract.

When we get down to the bottom of the stairs, I can hear several different men's voices. The deadly giant immediately takes a right-hand turn and leads me to the first door.

The voices are louder. I can tell he doesn't want to interrupt or maybe he just wants me to hear.

"We have the means to end him now. I've got several men in place, all he needs to do is step in front of the window or go outside, nobody will be able to connect it to us." A man with a nasal voice says, it sounds like he needs to quit smoking.

"I also have three men on Colt Moretti. He visits the same damn club every Friday night. We're ready for tomorrow. I got two different women as decoys in there waiting for him to get a drink. They have a vial that will end him." My breath hitches as I listen to this man I've never heard before talking about killing my brother. "When they realize their sister is missing, everything will go on lockdown."

I dart around my guard; he doesn't even try to stop me, and I bust into the room.

There are several men, five to be exact standing around Maxim, my next-door cheating fucking neighbor. *What the hell is going on, is he behind this?*

I walk fast up to the table, it almost looks like I'm stomping. "What the fuck is going on? And who the hell are you?" My previous plans of acting innocent and breakable fly out the freaking window. "Which one of you bitches want to harm my brother?"

None of them say anything. All of them are dressed exactly like my guard, khaki pants with a black polo shirt and black boots. They are big and muscular. Who the hell are these people?

All the men look between me and Maxim, not saying a word even their expressions are unemotional.

Maxim is giving me a cruel smirk, his eyes remain on me as he barks, "get out." The five men quickly exit and shut the door behind them.

"Sit down Anna," he speaks calmly like he didn't just freaking kidnap me, fuck someone else or listen to his men explain their plan to kill my brother.

I sit down in the seating area that I walked through to get to the desk. There's a leather loveseat and two leather recliners facing each other with a basic coffee table in between. I choose one of the recliners, keeping my distance.

Maxim goes over to his bar, pouring us both a drink. He hands one to me then sits down on the opposite side.

"You kidnapped me, was this planned all along?" The glass stays untouched in my hand as I ask him. I know I should be feeling fear or at least scared but right now I'm more confused and extremely pissed off.

He doesn't say anything, just swirls his drink around in his glass. His eyes narrow, they look deeper and darker. He looks mad at me. What the hell? Did I stab him in the neck and take him somewhere without his permission?

"What the hell is going on? I really liked you. I thought that for sure we had a connection. For fuck sakes, I was going to give my virginity to you. Instead, I get to walk in on you fucking someone else, actually scratch that. I need to be counting my blessings for what I *almost* did." I spit out the virgin comment cursing myself for not keeping my thoughts to myself.

His eyebrow lifts up, great he didn't know that, now I look more stupid. At least I look innocent because this situation is a whole lot worse than I could have imagined.

"I plan on killing your brothers, Mason and Colt, within the next few hours. Eventually, I will get to Jax and Finn, I'm saving you for last." He deadpans, then slams back his drink.

"Why would you want to hurt my family, is it because of me? I've done nothing to you." Saying the words out loud is making reality set in. Tears burn the back of my eyes as I realize I can't lose my brothers.

"It's something that your whole family has done. You all will pay for the loss that you caused me." Maxim gets up in a huff and quickly walks back to the bar refilling his drink.

I look down at mine, realizing I haven't even touched it. I slam it back hoping to calm myself down.

As he sits back down, I ask, "can you tell me why you want to hurt my brothers?"

"No," he spits out.

"Please, please don't do anything, I'm begging you." I

never beg anyone. My glass is put on the coffee table. I'm leaning on the edge of the recliner he has to know I'm serious.

Maxim studies me for a while gauging my reaction, most likely to see what I'm willing to do. "Are you willing to do anything? I would much rather get them all in one location."

"Yes, anything…. almost. I won't fuck you, who knows where that's been," I say. I sound angry and hurt, but I really don't want an STD. I have no idea how long I've been here, so they're not going to be on high alert. Anybody could get them.

Maxim leans back on the loveseat and unbuttons the black pants he's wearing. Lifting up slightly he slowly pulls them down his hips along with his boxers, letting his harden cock pop free.

My mouth waters. *Again, what the hell is wrong with me?*

He watches me, never taking his eyes off mine as he slowly starts to work himself up and down from root to tip. There's really no reason, he's already hard as a rock.

"If and when I fuck you will be my choice, you are my prisoner." He continues to stroke himself, my body starts to tingle just watching him. "Suck me off and make it good. Convince me you really want this, and I won't proceed today. I can't guarantee tomorrow but until then, they'll be fine. I'm a man of my word."

I take a deep breath this is what I wanted from him,

but not like this I wanted this connection the other night. Now it's just degrading.

I'm better than this, this will not get me down. I'm a fighter and I will figure out how to get out of this mess. I figure I've got twenty-four hours and still nobody knows yet what I can do, or I would have been chained down to the bed or at least handcuffed. I will save my family.

I slowly walk towards him and drop to my knees in between his legs. I reach out to grab him in my hand when he snaps, "no hands. Put them behind your back and if you even think of biting me, I'll make the call right now."

I nod in understanding. Maxim uses his hand to brush my hair behind my ear. It's personal, like something lovers would do, and it throws me off.

This is the only way! I repeat constantly in my head.

CHAPTER 13

*M*axim

"Let's go, I don't have all fucking day." She looks at me like she doesn't know if she's going to bite or suck. "Don't even scrape your teeth on my dick."

I don't think I could get any harder seeing Anna on her knees in front of me, her hands behind her back. Her eyes look pleadingly into mine. This is the perfect picture, I couldn't have painted one better myself.

I grip the back of her head and slam myself down the long narrow tube of her throat. "So tight," I growl as I swivel my hips, her mouth is fucking heaven.

I can hear her gagging, which doesn't bother me in the least. Moving my hips, I'm giving her a second to catch much-needed air before I slam back in over and over.

She had to have known what was going on. She and her whole family are killers, you can't just turn a blind eye.

"You might have bought yourself some time now, sweet thing, but I'm going to make you watch as I take down your brothers one by one." I tell her as I grab her head with both hands, pumping like my life depends on it.

Her eyes fill with tears, either from the gag effect or me letting her know what I'm going to do to her family.

"I might even share you with my men. There's only one reason you're being kept alive right now and that's for information. All this other shit is just an added bonus." I grab her hair in my fist, positioning her throat just right as I relentlessly pummel into her mouth.

She hasn't moved her hands at all, she's kept in the position I asked her to. And I am a man of my word, so I will wait and come up with a better plan. Most likely one that she can watch and be involved in herself when I take out her family, this makes me chuckle lightly.

My body tenses as I expel seed down the back of her throat. I haven't had an orgasm like that in a while, she's good. She was sucking and licking in all the right places.

Leaving Anna on the floor, I walk behind my desk tucking myself back in my pants. Now it's time to get to business.

Anna casually moves back over to the seat she was in originally, "who are you?" She asked as she wipes the corners of her mouth with her fingers then licks them clean.

Damn, I have to do this at least once a day with her. "One day you'll find out but right now it's of no concern to you."

She just watches me as I grab us bottles of water handing one to her. I may be an asshole, but I'm not that much of a dick. She did just give me one of the best blowjobs I've had in a long time.

"I have a couple of questions for you, and the way you answer depends on how easy this process is going to go for you and for your brothers." Total lie. I pull out a piece of paper and grab my pen, putting them in front of her.

Anna doesn't say anything, she just looks from me to the paper. "Write down all the names of the Moretti cases and any information pertaining to them that you can think of."

I honestly don't give a shit about this information. I want known connections with the Moretti family. What I do care about is the ones that might feel betrayed, the ones whose cases didn't go exactly as planned. These are the ones that can be blamed for the Moretti's death.

Anna bites her lip and starts to lean over the paper picking up the pen. I turn around smiling and walk back to my desk. It will be so much easier for her to work with me. It would take my people a few days and lots of resources to get this information.

After about a half an hour, she folds the paper and puts the pen down, "can I go back to my cell now?"

I nod my head. "Booker," I call out. "Please take Anna back to her cell." The girl snickers at his nickname. She doesn't spare me a backward glance.

I stroll over to the coffee table and pick up both the pen and paper. Cursing under my breath, I feel like punching a hole in the wall, but I'm more amused than anything.

Yes, there are lines and bullet points but every single word on this page is fuck you.

I sit down and lean back in my office chair throwing the paper on the desk. Damn, for something so small, she's a little firecracker. I don't know if I should be turned on or afraid.

Rubbing the three-day stubble on my face, I try to think of what to do next. Anna is my easiest and fastest link, I've got to get this information out of her.

There has to be somebody that doesn't like them as much as me. Someone needs to take the fall for what's about to happen to that family. Natural accidents are almost impossible to portray.

The door opens to my office and Booker comes in. The fucker sees that paper on my desk and picks it up, then starts laughing, throwing his head back.

I shake mine as he says, "I like this one. There's just something about her. She hasn't once asked me to let her go or call the police. Didn't even start the crying that all the other girls do. This one I think you'll need to be careful with."

"It's not just about being careful with her it's about figuring out the fucking information inside of her head. We might need to call in Carlos."

Booker shakes his head no. "That man is a psychotic butcher."

"Yeah, but he'll be able to get the information from her that we obviously can't get. We can have him go slow." I throw my hands in the air, "fuck man I don't want to do this. I don't like messing with women or children but what are our choices?"

"Not sure brother, why don't you just think on it for a few days." Booker suggests, "that girl doesn't look like much. You start fucking with her she might lock up for good, forever broken."

"You're right," I mumble to him as he gets up and walks out of the room. We're not sure exactly where his nickname came from, but his real name is Michael, he's been with me forever, my right-hand man.

We actually grew up together, his father worked for mine, there's nobody I trust more and there's nobody I trust with my life except that man.

I stand up and I grab the picture of the woman I'll never see again, and I whisper, "I'm sorry," before I set it back down.

I know Anna needs some isolation. Stuck in that room with nothing to do for days at a time can break the mind. Hopefully, by then she'll be spilling out secrets that I didn't even ask for.

Only time will tell.

CHAPTER 14

*a*nna

Booker walked me back to my cell in silence. I don't really feel like a prisoner, the house and my room are beautiful. Even the hallway I walked through had the most amazing thick carpet.

As soon as the door was shut, I could hear Booker lock it. For the first time since being here, I actually laughed. I can have that door open almost instantly, but what's on the other side? There could be fifty or a hundred guys that have guns. I could make a mistake thinking I could get away costing my brother's lives.

Ever since we walked back in the room, I've been feeling different emotions, relieved since I was able to get out of Maxim's office. Fear, because I have no idea what's going to happen to my family. Will I be able to get to them in time? And disappointment. I'm disappointed in myself because I actually enjoyed what Maxim made me do.

I enjoyed it way more than I should have. At the time, I wasn't even scared. I wasn't even thinking of my brothers, I was just thinking of making this man feel good and how he made me feel the other night.

Now is the time for me to plan. My ultimate goal is to get out, as soon as possible. With five guys, Maxim and Booker just in the office alone, I doubt I'd get lucky and that's how many are around the property.

This is going to have to be done silently, with me hidden. I'm going to need to escape with nobody knowing of my departure till it's too late.

I'm an optimist!

My virginity will come into play. If it's used to get me out of here, I honestly don't give a shit. I planned to give it to him anyway, just under extremely different circumstances.

First thing I need to do is find a weapon and maybe a change of clothes. I know the closet is empty and there's no dresser, so it looks like I'm screwed on that end. I would give anything for my own clothes right now.

I get up and quickly walk into the bathroom noticing the glass mirror. I can't use my fist to smash in the middle, that would be a dead giveaway. But I can smash off a corner.

The whole bathroom is covered in brown marble, even the countertops. There's no bathtub but the shower looks like it can fit 6 people, enclosed by a glass door. I would love to go in, but I don't want to be watched. I doubt if they would have a shower curtain on a shower as magnificent as that.

A real plant is on display at the other end of the counter. I wrap my fist in one of the towels right by the sink. I punch right against the edge of the bottom right of the huge mirror.

This is something my father taught me years ago when we were in a crappy hotel room. Before we really started making money.

The glass at the edges is weaker and you have less chance of it splintering if you need a quick weapon. This goes the same if you're trapped in a car. Kicking a passenger window at the top edge will crack more than something at the bottom or middle.

The punch works flawlessly, a little painful but it gave me a nice two by five-inch blade. If someone were to walk in this bathroom, they would totally be able to see that there's a chunk missing. I quickly grabbed the centerpiece and put it right in front, no one should be none the wiser.

I spend the next few minutes shredding pieces of the towel so that I can wrap one end into a good handle. Now, I just have to find a place to hide this, my gray skimpy pajamas aren't going to do it.

I spend the next several hours studying every nook and cranny, crack and crevice in this room. Under the bed, in the bathroom closet, in the bedroom closet and there's nothing I've missed.

I was able to slip my makeshift shank between the headboard and the wall. Nobody's ever going to look there, not even the maid that cleans this room.

Right as I finish, Booker and another man I've never seen before enter wearing the exact same khaki pants and Polo shirt. They bring in a tray of food and two bottles of water. Dinner time.

No words are said, they both just drop the items down on a two-seater table next to the closed curtains. I opened the curtains after I made my weapon. The beautiful window that spans the whole side of the wall points straight to another window that's part of the same house. If I had to guess, this would be Maxim's room. The room is twice the size of mine. I can't really see inside of it, I just have a feeling.

My privacy is already invaded, I don't want him looking in on me all the time.

The hours slowly start to drag by, as do the days. Usually, two men, Booker and another one, always bring me my food. Breakfast, lunch and dinner-the only time I don't get anything besides water is during breakfast, orange juice. I would kill for a freaking Coke, but I don't dare ask.

The morning of the fourth day, I'm about ready to crawl out of my skin. I smell and I smell bad. Two nights ago, I started switching off washing my pajamas and then the next night I would wash my underwear so I'm not totally naked.

But now hair is starting to grow everywhere, there is no razor in this room they probably think I'll use it as a weapon. I'm a religious shaver, I shave every day. I even thought about using the shank, but I'd just end up cutting my dumbass.

Now my mood is close to breaking, I'm lonely and incredibly bored. The door opens as breakfast is being brought in, but it's only Booker, maybe he'll talk to me.

"Why the fuck am I still here, what's going on?" Booker just looks at me, his eyebrows furrowing together. Shit, I need a play the weak girl, the breakable girl and not be such a bitch to someone I want something from.

"Please, tell me what's going on. It's been several days, and I don't know anything about my family, and my clothes stink." I whisper the last part looking down at the floor.

The beast of a man doesn't shut the door and lock me in, maybe he will talk to me, but all I see is a stone face with no emotion.

The giant leans his shoulder against the door frame. "Look, if you really want to get out of here and better your situation, you need to tell Maxim what he wants to know."

Booker seems sincere enough, but he is playing for the other side. "Is there any way I could get some clean clothes?"

He looks me up and down "I'll ask but I doubt it." He takes in a deep breath looking up at the ceiling. "Look, I like your no-nonsense attitude, you're not like the other ones that have been in here. You need to just stay smart and you'll get out of this."

That's the last thing he says as he the shuts and locks the door, trapping me back in my own personal hell.

Like the other ones that have been in here? Holy shit, is this guy kidnapping other girls?

He did have a point, I need to remain smart and active. Not reacting too soon.

It's time for me to up my not-yet-existent game. It's showtime Maxim.

CHAPTER 15

$\mathcal{M}$axim

I swipe my hand over my desk. "Fucking ridiculous," I snarl.

The Moretti's are like a locked box. And the person holding the key won't budge. I need to get a shit ton more information before I can move on.

It shouldn't have taken this long. I should be much farther along, hell I should be done. I need help.

I sit back in my chair on a long sigh. I'd rather punch the wall with my head fifty fucking times before I make this call, but I'm left with no other choice.

I use my cell phone instead of the landline. I don't want that little shit to see exactly where I'm at, that will just cause more problems.

"Maxim, it's only taken four months to hear from you," I can hear the malice in his voice.

"Dima, how are you doing brother?" I say with the little dignity I have left.

"Don't start the call with bullshit. You never call, so save us both time and tell me what this is about." He jumps straight to the point.

"You need to watch it, I can have you killed with just one phone call." Which is true, "I need you to tell me everything you know on the Moretti's. Especially any previous job contacts. I know that you're one of them." I growl out the last line.

"Don't start that shit Maxim, I am not afraid of who you are. I've seen you pee your pants." Dima snickers then continues, "I've been working with them closely and there's somebody on the inside. Listen, man, there was nothing we could do to save her, she was pretty much dead before we already contracted them out." Dima tells me, I know his heart is breaking, too.

"Both of us know that isn't true. If you would have just told me what was going on, I could have gone in there and got her instead of complete strangers."

"Oh, and you think that would have helped, guns-blazing going in there, they would have killed her instantly and got away." He states, most likely right. Dima is the most composed in our family. "I do have a present for you, well for both of us. The guy who had her all along is at our Bronx complex."

It takes me a minute to let the information sink in, "really?"

"Yes, but he will be given to you as an exchange

brother. I know you have the Moretti sister. Which is bad. You know they'll declare an all-out war with us. They could easily get the Italians, Mexicans and Irish on their side." Dima takes a deep breathe before he continues, "look, your family will be there for you no matter what, but you're giving us all a death sentence."

"Nobody knows I have her, you yourself were just guessing, so this conversation basically didn't happen. But either way, they do deserve to pay, even if there's an insider, I'll get him, too. The Moretti's shouldn't have fucked this up in the first place, this is on them.

"Okay, your word is law," he hisses. "I'll send you everything that I know."

"Thank you brother," I say then disconnect the call.

The Moretti's are a tight-knit group of people. The only way to get them to help with a case is a referral. Some of the higher up cases have been referred to them through the CIA and FBI. They say their noses are clean but that's all bullshit.

There's got to be more information available on them. I've never been this stuck before. I've always been able to get what I need but now there's a huge brick wall in front of me that's also encased by concrete.

Pulling my cell phone out, I send a message to Booker:

Me: Bring Anna to me.

This woman is more stubborn than anyone I ever met, I can't even begin to fathom how I'm going to get information out of her. I've got to play a game. She wants to know who I am and why I've taken her. I want the information on her family that's inside of her head.

This can be easy. I'll give something up when she gives something up. Damn, stubborn ass woman. Most of them would be crying or screaming or pleading or begging to be fucked or released. Every single one of them wanted something.

But not this one, Anna might not know who I am but still, that doesn't mean shit. Most people are afraid of just how I look and talk.

The door opens as Booker brings in a sashaying Anna. Confidence is very becoming for her.

Even in her disheveled state, she looks absolutely stunning, "please sit down."

She does as I ask, Booker quickly turns and leaves the room.

"You're most likely going to be here for a while, so I'd like to go over the rules with you. But keep in mind, if you share information with me, things will go so much easier for you, it might even save your life." I sit down behind my desk, not wanting to be too close to her.

She can see my reaction to her and smiles. "So, if I give you information, are you going to harm me or my brothers?"

Smart girl, "yes, they have to pay for what happened."

She leans forward on the chair. I've noticed she

always does this when she wants my full attention or when she's serious. "Let's just say, hypothetically that your whole story is wrong and everything that you thought happened isn't exactly the way it happened."

That would be an interesting twist, but not likely. "Well then, of course, I'd want to know. I'm not the type to go around hurting innocent people." I give her a glare letting her know I'm not talking about her. She is far from innocent, she did the research and the books.

"Well, until you give me some reassurance, I can't tell you anything. Would you tell somebody something that could hurt your family?"

"No." She's right, I would kill them first. Fuck, maybe that's what she plans to do to me.

I go over a few of the boundaries with her. The most important is she has to have somebody with her at all times. Not like it will really matter, she wouldn't be able to get away from here.

When we're done, I send a quick text to Booker to take her back to her room. I had my house attendant, Martha, get her some clothes so she's not wearing the same green pajamas.

Booker told me that she's been washing them in the sink. I could've been more of an asshole and locked the bathroom, or even kept her in the basement like my sister was. That thought makes me cringe.

In all honesty, it doesn't surprise me that she won't budge about her family, only the weak ones do, she has more sass in her than I originally thought. It's just going to be harder and take longer to break her down.

I don't have that much time. Her brothers will get wind of where she's at and launch a full-on attack to get her back. They won't win because I'm at an undisclosed location, nobody even knows that I have this property. I know I don't have a mole; my guys know I will kill them before I even can blink.

Booker arrives for Anna, and just like the other day she leaves without a backward glance. That woman is getting under my skin, it's starting to fuck with what I need to accomplish.

I get up and do the thing that she's been driving me to do more of lately, and that's head over to my bar and grab my favor decanter.

CHAPTER 16

*a*nna

I'm more excited about this day than I should be. I had trouble sleeping last night, too many thoughts running through my head trying to ram their way in all at once.

Today is the day for recon, even though I barely slept. I'm up early and ready in comfortable clothes. I would actually wear sweats if I had them but I'm more than okay with these black leggings and thick sweat-shirt I got on.

I know it's only around six in the morning at least that's what the alarm clock tells me. I pound on the door to let someone know to tell Booker that I'm ready. It's not like I have a phone to call him.

It takes almost fifteen minutes for him to show up. "Damn girl, you couldn't have waited till like nine."

I smile, "some of us have nothing better to do besides be locked up in a room, so why wait?"

We make our way towards the kitchen first. The huge property is fairly silent for this early hour, but Martha, the maid is there and she's already making us breakfast. Booker must have told her ahead of time.

She makes us a big spread of everything. We take our food at the breakfast bar and Martha joins us.

This is comfortable, it's inviting and relaxing. I'm able to learn a little bit more about her.

Martha was around when Maxim was a child, she's careful not to mention any other family names or the last name, it's like they're all hiding a big secret. She keeps reminding me that he was a great boy and now he's a good man.

There were a couple of guards that came in as we were eating. We were so silent they didn't hear us as they just shuffled on in.

"... Hey man, I understand you wanting to get with that chick, but she's all the way in LA. You honestly think she's going to come over three thousand miles here to New York to spend time with your ugly ass?" They both walk in, stopping in their tracks as they see me there, shocked.

Booker has a scowl on his face but doesn't seem too worried. They had to figure out I would eventually find out where we were. At least one problem is solved, now onto about forty-seven more.

After breakfast, both of us thank Martha then walk around exploring the different rooms in the house. There's a sitting room for men and one for women. A gift room, yes a place to wrap gifts. Booker told me there's a bowling alley in the basement, but I really didn't care to see it. I think the best I've ever bowled was a twenty-one.

The media room and the library are the ones I'm most excited about.

The guards, if they see us coming, walk in a different direction. I find it weird, like they're avoiding me, maybe there is something on my face.

It's probably what Maxim told them. I don't bother to ask Booker, he seems in a good mood and I want to keep it that way. Sometimes when I mention his boss, his brow creases, aggravating him.

The house is only two stories, but I found out that the property sits on almost twenty-five acres. The house is shaped like a horseshoe. This probably explains how Maxim and I are able to see each other when we open our windows. The only thing between us is a small courtyard.

The media room is divine. They have a way to access all new movies that are out. Of course, they probably pay an arm and a leg for it, it wouldn't even shock me if they just steal them. I definitely plan on visiting this room later if I'm allowed access.

The best room is the library, even for a non-reader they would be able to appreciate the art of this room. Books are stacked almost to the roof, with a ladder and rail system accessible for each and every title.

Every genre has its own area and that's broken up into smaller sections like romance, science fiction, nonfiction and more.

I'm not a huge reader but I do like to dabble, especially when there's nothing else in my room to do. So, this is my new most favorite place besides the kitchen.

I walk around and look at the different titles, that's when I noticed that Booker isn't right next to me. I look around for him and see him holding multiple books in his hand like he's borrowing from a library.

I casually walk over, "so you like to read?"

He looks at me and laughs, "don't be so shocked, I love to read."

It is a little shocking. "Normally someone that looks like you would rather smash heads instead of filling yours with knowledge."

Booker throws his head back laughing, "how do you think I got my nickname?"

My mouth opens, holy shit, *Booker*. I have a sudden urge to start giggling, but I stomp it down.

He nods with a twinkle in his eye giving me a devilishly sexy smirk.

"I grew up in a very good family, both of my parents were professors. I grew up on books, not video games, and not sports."

I hold up my hand, "wait a second, how did you end up built like a tank?"

He smiles, "when I got into college I discovered some sports that I really liked. It was history from there. My parents are awesome, they support me with whatever I do."

"Even kidnapping innocent women?" I cringe after I say that.

"Maxim's family is friends with my family. They know everything that he does isn't legit, but under that rough exterior he's a good man."

My feelings are all twisted for Maxim but even I shake my head. A man that wants to kill off a whole family is not a good man no matter what.

Booker and I make our way over to the ten ft tall stone fireplace. God this must be gorgeous when it's lit.

Right after we sit down to start looking through our books, his phone starts buzzing. He reads the message with a frown on his face and then looks at me.

"I need you to stay here for your own safety, just for a little bit. I shouldn't be more than a couple of minutes."

I nod this is ten times better than being back in the room. "I'll be fine, go do what you need to do." He quickly leaves and I get back into the dark paranormal thriller that I grabbed from the shelf.

After five minutes I need to find a bathroom, I drank way too much coffee at breakfast. There's nothing in the library but I'm pretty sure there's one right outside in the hallway.

It only takes me a couple of minutes to find one, use it, then back to the library.

A hand covers my mouth and squeezes, the same time an arm goes around my waist pulling me against a muscular body.

"I was told you were off-limits, but I don't see why. You're just like all the other bitches that come here." His voice is cold, and his breath is nauseating, like stale smoke and cheap whiskey.

I get ready to react, it's ingrained in me when out of the corner of my eye I notice Maxim and Booker walking towards the side entrance through a huge picture window in the hallway. They've got to be at least a football field away, so they haven't noticed us yet.

I take a shaky breath, as much that can be allowed through the hand covering my mouth. I almost made a monumental fuckup by taking him out.

I quickly drop to my knees, getting myself out of his hold screaming, "please don't hurt me."

The level of my voice shocks the hell out of both of us, it did wonders for me, not so much for this creep.

Maxim and Booker come running while the touchy-feely guy mutters 'fuck' under his breath.

I'm instantly lifted up into Maxim's arms, as Bookers slams the guy, I find out to be Troy, against the wall using his forearm pressed painfully to his neck.

"Are you okay," Maxim asks me as he looks me up and down.

Tears pool in my eyes, not from what just happened but from his concern, "yeah, I think so."

Maxim's sweet demeanor quickly changes to rage as he stands me up against the wall and stomps over to Troy and Booker.

CHAPTER 17

axim

The rage I'm feeling doesn't shock me, but why I'm feeling it does. Over a woman whom I plan to put an end to along with the rest of her family.

How dare that little fucker. I've had so much trouble with him ever since I agreed to his family to hire him on.

Troy has only been with me for two months, there have been a few minor incidents, but this is too damn far.

I just want to walk over there and snap his neck, maybe break up a few bones in the process, but I don't want to scare Anna. She's a strong girl, she might not even care, but still.

Fuck, what is wrong with me? Why do I care if she cares or not? I should terrorize her. I should set her right next to him and let her hear the sound of his bones breaking, the screams coming out of his mouth.

Troy had a smirk on his face as he was looking at Booker, then he caught sight of me... the smirk disappeared. Yeah, I can fuck him up, but Booker can also do the same damage. We were trained together, plus I know his guilt needs it more than me.

I give Anna a once-over just to make sure she's okay as I stomp over to that little fucker and grab him by the balls, squeezing just enough to get his attention but not too much so he can't have kids. This kind of trash shouldn't be able to reproduce anyway, maybe I'd be doing the world a favor.

"What did I tell you about Anna?"

He answers in a high pitch squeal, "she's off limits, but listen, boss, none of your bitches are off limits. What makes this one so perfect?"

I squeeze harder, making him scream out. "Because I fucking said so that's why."

Booker is fuming. Him and Anna have actually grown quite attached. I'll let him handle this. I know he wants the honor.

"Do what you need to do." I say as I look at Booker, "but don't kill him, the families won't stand for it."

He nods as I return to Anna, lifting her in my arms, cradling her. I decide to carry her up to my room but stop at the kitchen first.

She might want to be alone. I'll get Martha if that's

the case, but she shouldn't be, she can be traumatized or some shit like that.

I set her down on the bar stool. "Do you want to talk about it?" I ask as I go to the fridge and get her bottle of water.

She looks at me confused and then shakes her head. "I'll be fine, thank you for your concern, though."

Maybe it's time to let her know where I'm coming from. That I'm not this huge douche that she thinks I am. Not technically, I still want to off her whole family but that's the Ivanov way.

Looking at Anna, "I know this whole situation is fucked up, but your family made a mistake that resulted in the death of a woman that was a huge part of my family."

Anna whips her head to me. I can tell I shocked her talking about this. I figured she'd start throwing twenty questions at me, but she just stays silent and lets me continue.

"This should have been an easy job, nothing should have gone wrong. But your family messed up and they didn't take care of the situation, which cost her, her life." I want to rage just thinking that I'll never see her again.

Anna grabs my hand, "if you explain everything to me, then maybe I'll understand better, maybe I might even know what went wrong if it was with us."

I snatch my hand back, "it was with you guys. It might not have been with you personally, but it was

somebody the Moretti's hired or one of your brothers."
I start to walk, and Anna follows me.

She takes a deep breath, I know she doesn't want to argue with me, so I continue, "in my family, when something happens, you need to make restitution, an eye for an eye as people say. The situation needs to be paid for."

I watch her as she remains silent, "I wish we wouldn't have met this way. I wish we could have met under different circumstances, but this is how the world is, especially in my world and in my life. Nothing will bring her back."

She looks over to the curtain covered window back in my room now, "look, you may not think we're innocent. But I have no way to argue or convince you otherwise when you won't tell me the story. I have no idea how my family relates to your loss."

I asked her, "have you ever lost anyone you love? A family member that you would give your life for, like your parents or a sibling?"

"Yes, I've lost my Mom and grandparents when I was younger."

"That's what I've lost and that's why this is happening, not just to us but both of our families."

Anna grabs my hand again in a firm grip, "then you need to tell me the whole story, so I understand."

I'm shocked by this woman after everything I've threatened, plus the fact I've kidnapped her, that she still isn't shaking in my company, that she's wanting to hear me out.

"It's true you deserve the whole story." I was sitting on the edge of the bed, getting ready to explain to her about the woman that saved my life multiple times when the alarms in the house start to blare, this can only mean one thing.

We're under attack.

CHAPTER 18

*a*nna

The noise is deafening in the house from the alarms, it feels like I'm going through an elementary school drill. The ones that we used to have several times a year to get us ready in case of a tornado or other foul weather.

Maxim is up and running to the door, snapping at me to stay put. Excitement and disappointment are flowing through me at the same time. This could be what gets me out of here, but on the other hand, I almost got the whole story from Maxim why I've been imprisoned here for a week.

Booker and two other men I've never seen before, most likely lower level guards, come running in. Where do these people stay? It's like they're hidden just waiting to come out and save the castle. I guess that would make me the Damsel in Distress. I'm definitely no damsel and I sure as hell am not in distress, *I hope*.

I quickly sit back down on the bed. When the alarms started going off, I got up in my fighting stance ready to kick ass. My dumbass still needs to remember I'm the weak prisoner here and if they know I can fight, it's going to be really hard for me to get out of this place.

All of the men run out the door, I can hear Booker tell Maxim they're under attack. Maxim gives me a look that reminds me to stay in place as he closes the door and it automatically locks.

I am definitely not one to stay in place, especially if they're under attack from my family. I need to be out there fighting with my brothers.

This lock would normally hinder my response time of getting out but luckily I've been paying attention to everybody entering the codes on their doors.

It looks like they all have their own, probably shows when they go in and out of certain rooms. I have memorized Bookers and Maxim's-I use Maxim's to get out, quickly I punch in *11737*.

It opens without a problem. The hallway and the surrounding areas are filled with the voices of shouting men plus the occasional single gunshot.

I still have on my leggings and sweatshirt from earlier, but I don't have any shoes on. Most importantly, I don't have my knives which make me almost feel naked. I still excel in hand-to-hand combat, it just depends on whom I'm going against.

I need to sneak my way down to the kitchen but that's going to be almost impossible because that's where most of the voices are coming from, damn I need a knife.

The plush carpet keeps me almost invisible to any nearby ears. Adrenaline is starting to overthrow the disappointment and excitement previously coursing through my veins.

I slowly creep to the end of the hallway, as a man who must have been ransacking one of the rooms stands in the doorway, knowingly smirking at me.

I don't do anything, I just stand there and watch him. Is he a new hire? Is he with my brothers or someone else entirely? I decide to let him make the first move.

The man pushes a button on a Bluetooth device connected to his ears, "I got her at my location. Send backup, if she's here, they won't be far behind."

I barely make out the deep voice responding, "got it, Carlos."

The stranger is average build, with tan skin, dark hair and dark eyes. He starts to slowly circle around me. This causes me to turn, I don't want my back anywhere near him.

"You are a very hard woman to find." He states, keeping his distance. He must know that I can hold my own.

"Really? And exactly who is it that's trying to find me?"

He stops, which makes me stop. He isn't moving any closer just watching me. "It's not who it's what. The five-million-dollar price tag on your head makes you a very high commodity."

Shit, these guys aren't with my brothers. My brothers wouldn't offer a bounty, they would just come in and do it themselves. Who the hell has a bounty on my head?

Carlos can tell I'm putting it together and lunges at me, his hands are outstretched hoping to grab onto my neck or maybe my shoulders.

I don't give him a chance, I immediately pull my right shoulder back which tilts my whole body back-wards. The man stumbles a couple of feet past me, then looks right back with half a smirk and snarl on his ugly face.

"I see you like to play hard to get?" He asks as his whole body turns ready to make his next move.

I shake my head no, this is just another guy thinking he's playing a game with a weak and scared woman. I make sure to give my brightest smile letting him know I can play. Hopefully, he'll understand I'm gonna kick his ass.

He rolls his head around, making his neck crack. Like most men, he probably thinks this will be easy. It won't even cause his brow to sweat or his breathing to hitch.

I want to do the normal thing that most women are supposed to do and kick him right in the nards. This guy deserves it, but he'll be expecting it.

I shock us both when I use my right leg to kick the back of his left knee. I want to pummel his face, but he is too tall. I don't want to be throwing punches up.

The lanky man lands with a thud, then moans. This proves to me the marble floors are not very comforting.

I immediately throw an uppercut and then following the rhythm of left, right, left, right hooks.

I didn't hit him too many times. I don't want my knuckles all swelled up, even though I heard the bones in his face crack in several places. He lets go and seems to slowly float to the ground like the night I was stabbed.

I know it doesn't actually happen that way, it's dead weight falling down with a big thump on the cold and unforgiving hard marble.

I look down and my knuckles are light pink and a tiny bit swollen. There are blood spots all over my hands, that's the thing that's gonna bother me. Hopefully, Martha will bring me some ice tonight and by tomorrow my knuckles will be fine.

I start studying my fingernails, next to blood, dirty nails drive me insane. I can hear somebody clap behind me. A very tall dark and deadly man is looking right at me. His long hair is tied into a braid over his right shoulder. He is covered in tattoos: arms, neck, even his hands. The only place that looks clean is his face.

He's big and muscular, nothing like Maxim but I could tell he works out and takes care of himself. He stops clapping and just takes me in as I do the same. With my training, I think I'll eventually be able to beat him, but he looks like it would hurt a helluva lot.

"So sweet girl, does your captor know that you can fight like that?" He purrs. A deadly smile passes over his lips like he knows a secret I don't yet.

"I was protecting myself, that was just basics I learned in a woman's self-defense group." I can't lie for shit. Even this complete and deadly stranger can see right through me.

He laughs and puts both of his hands on his stomach making the muscles of his arms flex as he does a deep belly laugh. "I've seen fighters, and I know that you're definitely one of them. It's the way you punch, girl."

Fuck. All I need is trouble from this complete stranger. I need to get my ass back to the room. I give him my most evil glare, then start walking back towards the room I just vacated.

My arm is painfully grabbed as I'm spun around, "you're not going anywhere sweetheart, you're the woman of the night. The reason why we're all here."

CHAPTER 19

*a*nna
    His hand and meaty fingers nearly engulf my whole upper arm. He grabbed my left, big mistake. I'm about to punch him in the throat when I hear...

"Anna, it's time to leave." My fisted hand relaxes, and my fingers stretch out. Who is this man? How does he know my name?

Could he be working for my brothers? Maybe they decided to pay that much because they can't find me. Not true, they would be here with this group. This has to be someone else, maybe it's the stalker.

I yank my arm free from his hold, we're face-to-face, I need some damn answers now. "Who are you?"

The dark and deadly guy chuckles, "I'm Cruz. It's an extremely great pleasure of mine to meet you, Anna."

He holds out his outstretched hand for me to shake.

Is he kidding? I sigh in annoyance, "why are you here Cruz?"

"I'm here for you. You are the job." He pushes a loose tendril of my hair behind my ear. I want to punch him in the throat right now for touching me again, but damnit, I need more answers.

"Who hired you?" He's being evasive so I doubt he'll answer my question. "Was it my brothers?"

His hand moves down and grabs my shoulder, he tightens his hold to more than bearable, but not yet painful. "Your brothers are fucking idiots. If they paid attention to what info exists, and actually do their jobs, they would have been here before us."

Damn, it's got to be the stalker. I haven't hit anyone in the sternum for a while. Cruz still has a tight grip on my shoulder. I circle my neck, cracking it getting all the kinks out. At the same time, I extend my palm and get ready to plow right to his chest. But once again, I'm stopped by another voice.

"Cruz, let her go now, man. I've got you and all your bitches surrounded." Maxim, Booker and the two other guys from earlier come running up the stairs to us.

Cruz immediately lets go of my shoulder but doesn't leave my side. He stays close to the left side of my body, while Maxim and the others come over to the right.

"You know I can't let her go, Maxim. She's a five-million-dollar meal ticket." As soon as he says the last part, Cruz looks at me and licks his lips.

Great, am I supposed to choose between two psychos to go with? I've been locked up with Maxim forever and he's threatened to kill me and my whole family. Cruz hasn't threatened to kill anyone of us, but I get a very creepy and disgusting feeling off him.

I can't believe I'm even thinking this but staying with my current captor would be better than going with the one that's trying to kidnap me now.

Where the fuck are my brothers at?

Has Maxim covered up his tracks well enough not to be found? But, if that's the case, how was Cruz able to find me? Not trying to sound like we have big heads, well Colt does, but we're really good at our jobs. There's gotta be a reason they haven't moved in yet. Maybe they're just waiting for Cruz to get me out, then interject.

That sounds so stupid. They'd end up fighting just as much as they would now. We like to get in and out undetected. That's how most of our jobs go, yes there have been times where we've had to fight, sometimes multiple people, but that's not how we like to run things. Simpler is better, more complex can get messier and deadlier.

I can't even believe myself, that I'm about to do this. I move away from Cruz and stand behind Booker and Maxim with the other two newbies.

Cruz smiles at me, either understanding or thinking this might be a harder but more enjoyable competition for him.

He looks at Maxim, "you know I really like this one. She's got a fire inside her just waiting to come out. A little birdie told me that this was for revenge and I know you plan on getting rid of her." Cruz stops and looks at me, I keep my expression stoic, not letting them see anything. "How about instead we will make a deal? Maybe you would be willing to sell her to me?"

Maxim's breathing is going fast, kind of almost like a pant, but it sounds like a hiss. A very deep and deadly hiss. I move back a little bit away from him. I don't want to be this close when the shit hits the fan. The two newbie soldiers move in closer, flanking me on both sides with Booker and Maxim still in front of us.

"I'm not selling you shit, you're lucky that I'm letting you walk out of here alive and in one piece." I can see Maxim's hands start to open and close. His chest is heaving up and down. I can only imagine the view Cruz has. "You broke into my fucking house and killed three of my guards. Plus, let's not forget you tried to take something that is mine. This is far from over."

Cruz nods in understanding, it must be a boss thing. He turns his attention towards me, and his demeanor immediately changes. An engaging smile takes over his deadly face.

"Anna, this isn't over between us. I will be seeing you again, hopefully, sooner rather than later." He was looking around Maxim while he was talking to me. He nods, then turns around and heads for the stairs.

We all follow. It's like we need to see that he actually made it out the door with all of his men. At the top of the stairs overlooking the foyer, there have to be at least a hundred soldiers down there. It's a mixture of Cruz's and Maxim's men. Their guns are pointing at each other, waiting for anything. If someone accidentally pulls the trigger, it would be a blood bath.

All eyes turn to the stairs as Cruz naturally sways down. Not a care in the world.

We sit there and watch as they exit, nobody speaks or says a word for several minutes. I know this is a big and scary thing for them to have happen. Their house was invaded, just like mine was.

It puts you in a state of fear like you might never feel safe again. I want to point out they did this to me, but now's not the time for me to go running my big mouth.

CHAPTER 20

Maxim

I watch until every single one of Cruz's men leave. Then I stand there just for a few minutes longer to get myself under control. Me blowing up right now would not do anybody any good except maybe scare the shit out of Anna.

I cannot afford a war with the Mexican cartel now. Cruz should be dead, he broke in my house, *killed* my men. He will one day pay for this, and he knows. He also knows I had to let him walk out of the house. *Fuck.*

I reign in my temper as I look towards Anna and ask, "are you okay?" She nods slightly unsure.

If we didn't arrive at that exact moment, he could've got her out of the house. Who the hell knows who put that bounty on her? I sure as hell know that it wasn't her brothers, they would do the damn job themselves.

I look at Booker and the other two men that nod

towards Anna. "Take her back to her room." All of them start to walk down the hallway, "then come and meet me in my office. Make sure the outside is locked so no one can get into her room." This is just an extra precaution in case her or someone else knows the regular codes to open the electric lock.

I quickly walk down to my office, sharing a few glances with some of my men. Martha is running around like crazy trying to help everyone she can. I don't need to tell her to call the on-call doctors. We've been down this road before.

There are three of my guys that are laying under white sheets just off of the foyer. I can't look to see who it is right now. I'll have Booker give me an update later. We will make sure their families are well compensated and cover the funerals.

I get into my office and sit behind my desk, my fingers rub my temples then push on my closed eyelids. I can feel a headache creeping in.

I want to relieve this anger and start punching the walls. I have an overwhelming urge to break every-thing apart that's in front of me. I know this is what my men are expecting and why most of them are avoiding me. This will solve nothing, it will only delay us getting to the bottom of this faster.

Booker comes in as the other two men stand guard outside. He must've picked them himself, he always likes to grab one or two of the new guys and show them the ropes independently. He's always wanted to be a teacher. If I can't find him, I know just to look in the library.

Booker takes a seat on the opposite side of the desk from me. I ask him, "who the fuck would want Anna so bad to pay five million?"

"No clue brother." Booker just shakes his head.

"I know it's not the Moretti's. The brothers would just come here themselves and take care of this. They'd do it smarter, probably taking one of my siblings and asking for a trade." I shake my head as it hits me, "they don't know that I have her."

Booker nods, "I don't think they do. But, my question for you is, how did Cruz know?"

"That's what we need to figure out," I start to tap my fingers on the desk. There's a piece that we're missing here. "Maybe Anna will know something more about this. I was gonna set up a previous client to take the fall for the demise of the Moretti's, maybe there is actually another client who hates that family as much as we do. Or it's someone in love with that girl?"

Booker rubs the stubble that's slightly growing on his chin with his thumb and forefinger. "Have you thought about somebody on the inside?"

"Yes, I have, but none of it adds up. If we did have somebody working on the inside here, they would've been able to pull this off. This wasn't for us, they were actually coming for *that* girl."

Booker and I both just sit in silence for a while thinking over possibilities and scenarios. When both of us get our heads together, we actually do pretty well. There hasn't been a problem yet, we haven't been able to solve.

"How do you think they penetrated the compound?" I look at Booker and watch him as he contemplates his answer.

"I believe it was just pure luck and coincidence. Two of the guards got into an altercation earlier and several others decided to form a circle around them. This left areas not as heavily guarded. That might sound like a convenient setup but it's not. They've been at each other's throats for the past five years and one of them just got sick of it. They both have been removed from their positions today."

I get up and head over to the bar bringing the decanter and two glasses back with me. Sometimes Booker decides to drink but it's very rare. I just set his glass down in front of him and fill my own.

Booker is lost in thought, he never even notice the glass sitting in front of him. He turns to me then says, "just to be on the safe side, we need to go through the video. All the footage we have on the compound just to make sure nothing looks out of place, that no one looks out of place."

"I'll get started on that. There's not that much video, they were here less than thirty minutes." I start to power up my laptop, "why don't you interview the men. See if anyone seems a little shady or if they're acting weird. Have someone you trust go back and interview the two that started the fight earlier just to be safe."

"Got it, boss," Booker says as he gets up and heads out the door.

I spend the next three to four hours going through every angle that we have in the house. Making sure that no one looks out of place. I don't have cameras in a few places, one is a hallway where Anna's room is located and the other one is where my room is located. Cameras need to be installed there right away. I'll never put them in the bathrooms.

No one is out of place, and no one is acting weird. The only problem that I've had are the two men that started the fight earlier. I don't even know what the fuck they were fighting about, probably a woman or money. But it was expected for Booker to fire their asses. They're lucky he didn't put a bullet in their empty heads.

Booker comes back into the office after he's interviewed everyone.

"Not one thing is out of place boss. Several of the men were anxiously fuming. I sent them home to relax. They're pissed and can't believe that the compound was attacked during their shift and on their watch."

I smile, these are the type of guys we need. "Did you get to interview those two that started the fight."

"Yep, everything is good. They wouldn't stop apologizing to Mark and Jackson. Those were the two guys I sent over there." Booker and I both smile, we know that they are not going to be a problem later on.

The sun starts to shine through the open office window, we've been at work all night and I'm fucking exhausted. I stand up and stretch. Even though that shouldn't have happened last night, I couldn't have asked for a better outcome, besides losing my three men. I had no traitors on the inside.

Booker leaves the office at the same time I do. We both head towards the kitchen. Martha is already in there cooking breakfast for everyone, God I love that woman.

I grab two plates and give her a kiss on the cheek. I can feel the exhaustion as I make my way up to Anna's room. Maybe she has some insight to whom the hell broke into my house last night.

I balance both plates on one arm as I lightly tap on the door. I can hear her small voice whisper, "come in."

Anna is up and dressed, just sitting on the bed, staring at the wall. Maybe I should bring a TV in here.

"I thought you might want some breakfast." I stroll over to the table for two and set both plates down, hoping that she'll join me.

"Thank you, I'm starving." She's already seated and shoving food in her mouth before I have a chance to finish sitting down.

I lightly laugh and take my time eating as I just watch her thoroughly chew and swallow every bite. It seems like we haven't fed her in over a week. Maybe I need to check and make sure they are feeding her, or this girl just has a damn healthy appetite.

She finishes her plate of bacon, eggs and hash browns then looks longingly at my toast. I don't even ask if she wants it, I smile pushing it towards her. I'm not that hungry this morning, it's probably because I haven't slept.

I stare at Anna's beautiful face. Her hair is piled up in a messy bun on top of her head. She's wearing the leggings that she usually likes with a really thick over-sized sweater. The woman is absolutely gorgeous, even eating like a pig.

"As you know, people broke in the compound." I start talking to her like a conversation where I'm sharing details. I'm hoping she'll be honest with me because I don't like not knowing how someone knew she was here and got into my house. "I'm pretty sure they're not affiliated with your brothers."

She takes a drink and then chuckles, "I'm definitely sure that's not my brothers' work. That's not their style and they don't need to pay five million to rescue me."

"I agree. I also believe they don't know where you're at, so there is someone else that's not currently in this equation." I try not to smack her in the face with the facts right away, but there's no time to waste and I sure as shit don't have time for sensitivities.

Anna drops her newly butter toast back on the plate, "I don't think they know where I'm at, either." She bites her lip for a little while contemplating if she's going to tell me more. "I've had a stalker for over a year." She says as she looks down at her buttered toast.

That immediately has me sitting up straighter, "a stalker? Like someone that follows you around and looks into your windows?"

She shakes her head, "no, like someone who sends me creepy gifts with weird messages."

"Like what? This is been going on for more than a year?"

She nods and then tells me about all the different kinds of roses and lingerie. Plus, different pictures that have been taken of her and her family. "I kept a box with the original notes and pictures of the items in my room."

I study her face, I can see this upsets her. I don't want to keep asking her questions on the subject. "I'll have a couple of my men go retrieve the box and make sure your place is okay, and to see if any other packages have been left."

All she does is nod, she doesn't even make eye contact with me. Anna picks back up her toast and starts to eat it. I need to leave this alone now.

I go stand behind her bending down, whispering, "don't worry, I'll find out who it is." I leave the room and head to mine. I need to sleep.

We sure as hell will find out who it is. With this new information, I'm pretty positive Anna's stalker is the reason I had the Mexican cartel in my house. Nobody gets away with that shit.

CHAPTER 21

*a*nna

When I can't leave the room during the day, it's absolutely lonely and desolate. Ever since Maxim left, I've just been moping around.

I don't have much time.

Those words shouldn't bother me as much as they do, but I actually feel a connection with my captor. I've been here under two weeks, but it feels much longer. All I want to do is hang out with Maxim and maybe go to the library with Booker.

Never in my life has another man affected me this much, ever. I feel like a giddy schoolgirl with a crush and if he looks my way I just might explode.

I have to devise a plan where I control my future, nobody can do that for me. Since I don't know who my stalker is, I could end up in some mad man's house worse than Maxim and even that lowlife Cruz.

The time has come for me to leave. I need to figure out what Maxim's connection is to my family, and one of the most important things, who Maxim actually is. This man is an absolute enigma.

With the help of my brothers, I also need to figure out who my stalker is. This one should probably be the most important, but my fascination with Maxim leads all.

I look around the boring old room. I've been dressed and ready since Maxim came for breakfast. My body just tingles in delight every time I think of that man.

The alarm clock on the end table shows that it's two PM. I wonder if seven hours is enough time for him to sleep. I need to get my plan moving and actionable now.

I left a permanent mark on the carpet, I've been pacing since that man left at seven AM. One of the guards dropped by lunch a couple of hours ago but that's all the interaction I've had with anyone today.

Several books would be freaking nice. When I go out today, I need to grab some or I'm gonna go insane. I start to pace faster, nerves are getting the best of me which I can't allow. I am never this wound up. I need to get my head into job mode, that's the only way this can work.

Maxim has to become the bad guy, which in all honesty he really is, but one that I can't keep my stupid brain and heart from, damn hormones.

Okay, Anna get it together!

Now for my plan, absolutely nobody in this house will help me. At first, I thought I might be able to turn Booker or at least get him to sympathize with me. Maybe he could just look the other way for a couple of minutes. Now I know there's no way in hell that will happen, he is very loyal to Maxim.

All the guards seem to be. I don't know if that man overpays or they just have a sense of severe loyalty to him, who knows. I don't have enough time to stick around and find out.

I even thought about asking Martha for help, but she's like a mother figure to these boys. I think she would kill me herself before she betrayed them.

So, it comes down to just little ol' me. My best plan is to get him in a vulnerable position. It has to be in the middle of the night, the guards are a lot thinner in numbers. Which to me makes no sense, I would attack in the middle the night.

Maybe they just want me to think that. Maybe they're all standing by and really hiding in plain sight. Okay, now I'm overthinking everything again. Keeping my wits about me will get me out of this.

I look over by the door and spot my Birkenstocks. These people have heated floors in some of the areas, but they are still cold on my bare feet.

I slip on the shoes and make sure that my bun is still up on my head, I can't stand stray hairs on my face, and I enter Maxim's code to open the room. The door opens for me instantly, almost taunting me towards my freedom. I imagine Maxim was too tired to put the outer lock on.

Exactly what am I gonna do today? When I walked around the property at this time on other days, I've spotted at least thirty to fifty men. I know my ass can't take on that many.

Walking down the hallway towards the stairs, everything seems just like a normal day. Voices of men, some are laughing, some arguing. They always walk around in twos. The only time I've ever ran into a single guard was when Troy attacked me.

As I make my way down the stairs, I can hear my Birkenstocks clack on the wood. I bet the tone is different on the marble.

My brain is starting to fry from boredom if I'm wondering what tones are sounding like. I can see guards stationed at the bottom of the foyer by the front door and a few outside through the windows. Some of them nod in my direction, while others don't even pay me a second glance. They must be as used to me as I am to them.

When I reach Maxim's office, I see that his doors open and it's dark. He must've not gotten up yet, but the doors always closed, even when he wasn't using it.

Feeling frustrated, I turn around to head towards his wing of the house when I smack right into a solid chest. "Sorry," I mumble out before I look up and see Maxim staring right back at me.

I guess he is up. He smiles warmly, "what are you doing down here?"

I shrug, "I'm bored out of my mind." I don't want to add that I know all of your codes even though he probably knows. My luck, they would all be changed tomorrow and then I would be stuck. It would be hard to explain how an innocent and naïve girl was able to pick a lock, even an electric lock.

Maxim nods towards his office, "come in, there's something I want to tell you about." This can't be good.

I follow him in and sit down at my usual spot across from his desk, more room and space that way. The tingles are already flowing through my body. I feel at any second they're gonna lift me off my feet and plummet me right towards him. It'd be really hard to explain why I'm straddling the man.

Maxim puts his elbows on this desk and interlocks his fingers. "There was another package left for you." He just looks at me waiting for my reaction.

My head shoots up as I stare at him, "really? Can't even give a kidnapped girl a break for a little while?" That makes me laugh. Even my stalker can't leave me alone when I'm dealing with a family emergency. Well, the emergency being that the man in front of me wants to kill all of us.

Maxim smiles looking at me like I might break down in tears, I hate pity smiles. "Your apartment was also broken into. That box of pictures and the cards were taken."

Damn, "that really sucks." Thinking about it for a minute, I knew I should've given them to one of my brothers. "I do have pictures of all the cards and the items, but it's not as good as the real thing. They are on my phone," that you stole from me. I wanted to add but I kept my mouth shut.

"Everything helps," Maxim reassures me. "That's a whole lot better than having nothing at all."

"Was anything else taken or destroyed?" I don't have that many personal items, and most of the stuff I keep it the main Moretti house. That box was the most important thing I owned as of now, but it still bums me out someone went into my private space and vandalized it.

"They tossed the place around, but it looks like it was a professional clean hit." Maxim and I both hear a vibration. He pulls his phone out of his pocket and checks what looks like an incoming text message. "I have a few phone calls I need to make."

I can take a hint, that's my cue to go, but I still need to work on my plan, and it needs to happen within the next day or two. "I was wondering if you wanted to have dinner tonight or tomorrow night?" I spit it out.

Maxim looks stunned for a brief second but then relaxes. "I would love to. Tonight, won't work, I've got several conference calls, but tomorrow we can have a nice dinner in the dining room."

"That would be great! See you tomorrow." I say as I get up and practically run out of the room. I have barely any experience with men. I definitely don't have experience with kidnappers, unless my Stockholm syndrome's taken effect.

I slowly make the trip back up to my room, no reason to hurry. At least one thing is checked off my list. Now I have until tomorrow to make a good enough plan to pull this off.

Tomorrow night I will lose my virginity, but I will also gain my freedom and I'm not upset about any of this.

CHAPTER 22

*M*axim

I watch as the beautiful Anna rushes out of my office. Things are progressing very weird for both of us. The woman that I planned on killing a couple of weeks ago has been inching her way into my heart.

I smile at all of her weird ass traits. I've never met anyone like her. More and more over the days I've been thinking if only the situation was just different.

What exactly would I do if we met on the street? All I'm ever up for is a great night, not multiple nights. I don't want to be tied down to one single woman. Maybe I just haven't met the right one and of course, it happens to be the one whose family is the reason my sister isn't alive today.

All I really want to do is go over to the bar and start drinking again, that never solves anything except sending me to bed early and making me into a bitch the next day. Those are Booker's words, not mine.

Right before I laid down after having breakfast with Anna, I received a call from a couple of my men. Apparently several guys from what looks like the Mexican Mafia broke into Anna's place.

I told them not to interfere, even though there was a good chance they would take that box I was looking for. I'm determined to figure out who her stalker is.

They just sat and watched them go through the place on video. I had them install cameras right after we took Anna. I figured we needed to see if her brothers were coming around, which they did.

They were in and out in less than five minutes. They were just looking for signs of life and nothing else. They know that nobody knows about this place, this is Anna's secret apartment, well nobody except for us and now obviously the Mexicans.

We've been having her followed for a long time, which makes me believe the Mexicans have somebody on the inside like Anna was afraid of.

I need to talk to her later about her past relationships, maybe there's a clue there.

I pull up my laptop and start to playback the video that I haven't yet watched of the men at Anna's house. All the information I related to her I got from my guys earlier. This is the first time I've had a chance to watch this.

They are very meticulous and go through everything, but they don't damage too much. Maybe that box was the intended purpose they were there in the first place, but I also believe they were looking for her location.

They are in and out in under fifteen minutes, after several minutes the coast is clear. I can see my guys coming in to survey the damage, even though they already watched the video.

We also have video surveillance at the Moretti cabin. These men never even showed up, the brothers did. Just like at her private apartment, they were in and out in under five minutes looking for signs of life.

Even the stalker had changed the package destination and moved them over to her apartment. If I were to be a betting man, I'd put all my money on someone that knows her. Maybe someone that's even close to her but she's not returning the same euphemisms to him.

One thing that's been on my mind ever since this morning, what if the Moretti's found the package before we did? I don't think it would really matter if the Mexicans found it, because they're most likely working with the stalker. What kind of twisted world would this open up, if they found this package before us? As a brother of now only one living sister, I would be pissed if she didn't tell me.

I open the bottom drawer to my desk and pull out the newest package that was left for Anna. I didn't give her any of the information on it. I don't want her to worry about it anymore, I just need to find the sick creep. Get rid of him or instead, just let the brothers deal with it.

They're protective like I am for my siblings, that's why we're in this whole fucked up situation in the first place. Anna would probably get her ass kicked at the same time the stalker did for not talking to them. She did mention to me that this has been going on for over a year, that's a long ass time.

We carefully opened the package earlier. There's pair of handcuffs in here, white leather. I'm not sure if this would freak her out if I told her.

The card is laid neatly on top. It's just a white stock index card and the message has been printed.

Looks like I need these when I finally get my hands on you. My dear Anna, you haven't been keeping the best company.

The last part is most likely a reference to me. The stalker has to be somebody higher up in the ranks of one of the families. There are just too many connections and coincidences here.

I carefully rearrange the package the way it was, placing it back in the drawer. I'm going to have to show her what it was later. Before I close the drawer, I take out her cell phone and start to go through the many different pictures and messages.

There's gotta be a clue in here somewhere that points to something someone might've seen. Even a connection between the different florists that were used, or the delivery service would be a big help.

I send every picture from Anna's phone over to Booker. I want him to start working on this right away. The sooner this problem goes away the sooner I can get back to figuring out what I want to do with her and her family.

I know I'm not gonna kill her now. The brothers most likely won't share the same fate.

I think I might just keep her and make her mine. It's not like I've never done anything this bad before.

CHAPTER 23

*a*nna

The morning of our date night, Maxim sends me a huge gift box. Before the stalker, I used to love to get presents. I was the one that was jumping up and down every Christmas morning. Waking up my brothers and my parents before the sun even came up.

I'm actually excited again because I know this is a nice present, it's not a present from a creep. I can't believe I just thought that. I don't know that much about this man, even though he did tell me he was gonna kill me and my family. I just don't get bad vibes from him.

My thoughts and emotions are all twisted and screwed up. I don't even know what direction is up, what's the right thing to feel anymore? I need to just keep going like I've always gone and that's with my instinct.

I decided right then and there that I'm not gonna make any decisions on this man until I hear his side of it. It might not be the answer to the question I'm looking for but at least it'll be something.

The package he sent requests my presence in the dining room exactly at seven PM. Inside is a beautiful emerald green silk dress and a pair of black Louboutin's, both items are in my size.

I'm ready by six thirty PM. I just sit on the bed, this would be the time I pick up my cell phone and call a girlfriend. We giggle and talk back and forth. Maybe I would call and get advice from my mom about how to act and what not to do tonight.

I don't have any girlfriends that would engage in this conversation with me and my mother's been gone for eleven years. I quickly start to blink the tears away that are welling up in my eyes. Damnit, I spent a while on my makeup.

My mother passed away when I was twelve years old. Some days it's like I can barely remember her, and others I remember almost everything.

I was very jealous of my brothers. They got her longer than I did. It almost broke my father, he slowly was able to pull himself out of his deep depression with the help of us and other family members.

My mom died from ovarian cancer, we never knew she had it. She didn't even know she had it until it was at stage four. She went to the doctor for severe cramps, and that's when they found it.

She was stubborn and one hundred percent Italian.

Mom died five weeks later. A lot of people tell us we should be grateful she didn't have to suffer for long. Some people go through this for years.

None of us were grateful, we just wanted our mom back.

I quickly fix my makeup. I'm all alone in this. But, I damn well know I'll make it out. I've got Moretti blood running through me.

With five minutes to spare, I get up and go over to the door. I lightly tap, I should probably try to follow some of the rules.

It's opened by a younger guard I've never met before, he has kind eyes. He gives me a low whistle and holds out his arm to escort me to the dining room.

"You look very nice, ma'am," loaded with charm and he talks just like a good southern boy with excellent manners.

"Thank you," I reply as I grab onto his arm, we start to walk towards the dining room.

No more words are spoken but a lot of heads turn as we walk by. Some of the men give me polite nods and smiles, while others just leer at me, they even gawk and ogle.

Well, this isn't uncomfortable at all. My chaperone holds out the chair for me as I sit down, and he pushes in the seat. Maxim takes a moment to enter the dining room. The guard nods at him then gives me a cheeky grin as he rushes out of the room.

Maxim takes my hand, "you look absolutely stunning." So, does he. He's dressed in one of his tailor-made Armani suits. His hair is still his messy style, but I love it when it's that way.

He's wearing a blue satin tie that makes his eyes pop out more. Maxim takes a spot next to me at the head of the table. Right as he sits down, waiters start bringing out our first dish. It's a salad loaded with hard-boiled eggs, meat, cucumbers and spinach. Don't forget the extra helping of ranch. He's been paying attention to what I like.

Maxim's salad looks divine and very expensive, kind of like something you would get in a fancy restaurant. Well, at least the serving size of it. It's on the same size plate as mine but it looks like only five or six spinach leaves with some fancy cheese and croutons, topped with a clear vinaigrette. I'm very happy with mine.

The sexual tension is off the charts by the time the main course finishes. I don't even pay attention to the food anymore. I know that we did have soup. I think the main course I ate was lobster and steak. Whenever we would break from eating, Maxim would reach out his hand and caress mine.

It's the sweetest and most erotic thing I've ever felt. I just want to switch over to being left-handed so I can keep my right hand down for him to constantly hold. He keeps doing something with this thumb going in circles and then using his fingertips to barely, glide over my hand. I might jump him right here.

I declined dessert even though it was tiramisu. I can't push anything else into my body. When Maxim finishes his dessert and the waiters clean up the table, he gets up and goes over and gets us a drink.

The same thing is always served. I rarely drink, so I really don't know what to ask for, plus I don't have a preference. Three to four fingers of whiskey neat is put in front of both of us.

My nerves are on high alert right now. I just take the glass and slam the whole thing back. When I put it back down on the table, I can hear Maxim chuckling next to me. He knows, his eyes never leave mine.

The atmosphere is so relaxed, besides the sexual tension. I almost pulled another dumb move and asked him again about our connection. Thinking that now would be the time to talk about it.

The only thing that would lead to is ruining the mood and nothing would happen. Tonight, is when I'm determined to leave. It must be about eight o'clock right now I should be back home within six to seven hours.

That makes me excited but not near the same amount as the raging butterflies in my stomach.

Maxim stands up and grabs me by the hand, pulling me to my feet. His body presses against mine as his arms circle around me pulling me as close as I can get to him.

I can feel his need for me on my stomach, which makes my nipples pebble. He runs his hand up and down my back, causing the silk dress to lift up. The silk feels wonderful on my skin.

I can't wait any longer. I grab him by his jacket lapels and smash his face against mine, our lips press together. He groans out and I open my mouth, allowing him access.

I'm immediately lifted up on the dining room table and my legs are spread open. He pushes until he's completely flat against my core, finding the right spot. He moves his hips as he takes my mouth with no mercy.

I moan, trying to pull him closer to me it's like I just want to climb up him. I can't get enough.

Instantly the kiss is broken, and I'm pushed back hard, which causes me to grunt. My back is on the dining room table and my knees are bent as my feet are pressed on the table right next to my backside. The silk dress pools at my waist.

Maxim leans down next to my core and inhales deeply. I want to be embarrassed but I'm not. I'm so freaking turned on, he can probably even see the wet spot on my panties.

They don't stay there very long. Using his hands, he rips the panties in half and throws them to the side. I can hear him groan as he looks at my aching need.

Maxim licks his lips and smiles as he leans down using both thumbs to spread open my pussy lips. I know I need to hold onto something, I've only have this done once and it was horrible. So far this is a hundred times better.

I ball the silk dress in my hands on my stomach and hold on tight. I hope that my feet don't slide off. My knees are already going weak with anticipation.

"Relax Anna," Maxim says as he presses his tongue right in my hole, he licks up then latches on to my clit, sucking and doing delicious things, twisting and teasing.

A finger enters me slowly and starts to work in and out. I gave myself orgasms before but this one feels like I'm just gonna blow apart, its building and building.

Another finger is added, the rhythm goes from slow to fast, he's pumping hard. His tongue never leaves my clit for second as his other hand moves up and pulls down hard on the front of my dress, ripping the gorgeous gown right in half, exposing my breasts. The cool air makes my nipples impossibly harder.

All the sensations have me crying out as my orgasm rips through me. July forth has nothing on this man. New Year's Day doesn't have anything on him. Maxim can open up his own fireworks shop.

My body tenses as I allow the sensations to flow through me. At first, I thought it was gonna be too painful. It's freaking divine, glorious even.

Maxim stands up and licks his mouth with his tongue. He sucks me off of his fingers. "I want to fuck you, but not in here." I nod a little bit more than I should. I really want him to fuck me right now, too.

Maxim helps me down from the table and he gives me a searing kiss. When he pulls away, he puts his jacket around me, never taking his eyes off of my boobs. There is no way to wear a bra with the dress.

He lifts me up in his arms, "I'm taking you upstairs to my room." Yes, please yes.

CHAPTER 24

*a*nna

Maxim rushes us into the room and drops me on the bed. He stands there and just looks at me for a few minutes as I take in my surroundings.

This is the first time I've been in this room, it's much bigger and more masculine designed than mine. Everything is just brown and black, I never thought those colors would work well together, but it does.

His room is set up the same with the doors and the long wall with a curtain. I want to go over and open that curtain just so I could see if my room is facing me. The one main difference is he's got an eighty-five-inch TV mounted on the wall in front of the bed between two doors, which happened to be one of the doors we came in through and the other the bathroom.

On the left is his walk-in closet. The doors are open, right in plain sight is my gear bag. I gasp, quickly swallowing it. Turning my head to Maxim, he's over at his dresser, which is a cherry oak wood. He's taking the stuff out of his pockets and is putting it on the dresser.

I know he's taking his time to give me a chance to change my mind, but now after seeing my bag, I have to act tonight. *Am I ready?*

After what happened in the dining room, I am still so turned on I get chills just thinking about what he did to me, for me. While his back is facing away from me, I quickly take off all my clothes.

Finding a sexy position on a bed for a virgin is not very easy. After trying several, I just lay with my legs crossed and look up at the ceiling.

The bed tips right beside me as Maxim trails his fingers over my exposed skin, never hitting any of the places I want him to. "Are you sure?" He asks.

I nod my head. Even though I'm leaving tonight, I definitely want this more than anything. Grabbing his hand that's trailing over my rib cage, I bring it up to my mouth, inserting two of his fingers and start to suck on them.

That sets him off in a frenzy. He stands up quickly and rips off his clothes. I watch, taking in his body, he's absolutely beautiful.

Maxim positions himself in between my legs. "I'm going to try to go slow since it's your first time, just let me know if I'm hurting you." His lips come down to mine as he gently takes me in a sweet kiss, while his cock slowly pushes in my never before entered sacred place.

He keeps kissing me, distracting me, massaging my breasts and tweaking my nipples while he slowly pushes inside. Suddenly, he pauses and looks at me in the eyes making sure I'm ready. I don't move to stop him as his hips thrust forward, stronger than I thought was ever possible.

I scream out in pain, as he just took my virginity.

"Are you okay?" I nod blinking away the tears from my eyes. I didn't think it would hurt this much.

Maxim slowly moves just to get me used to this feeling and I'm grateful for that. After a couple of minutes, the pain subsides, and pleasure starts to build.

I grab the cheeks of his ass and try to push him harder. I can hear him chuckle as he starts to fuck me faster. He keeps caressing and kissing while thrusting.

He's making love to me.

Maxim wraps his arms around me, bringing us both higher and higher. I know I won't orgasm this time, I still have a dull pain. I actually read somewhere only a very small percentage of women do on the night they lose their virginity.

But, he more than made up for it earlier. Maxim's whole-body tenses and I can feel the warmth of him exploding inside of me.

Shit, we didn't use a condom.

Maxim pulls out and goes to the bathroom to get a rag and starts to clean me up. "Are you on the pill?

That's never happened before, I always use a condom. Just so you know I'm clean."

"No, not on the pill, but I get a shot every six months for cramps, so we're good." He smiles.

Maxim lays down beside me and puts my back to his chest, covering us both up. I guess I'm sleeping in here tonight.

I can feel his breathing even out, it only took him a couple of minutes to fall asleep, I glance over to his alarm clock on the nightstand. It's already two in the morning.

I wish things didn't have to be this way. I wish we could have kept on dating and got to know each other better. That I wouldn't be captive in his house.

I will never take back having this experience with him and having him be my first, but because of the situation, that's all we'll ever be to each other. He's out for revenge, which I still don't know why and me trying to protect my family.

The tears start to come now, but I've been able to master crying silently. Yes, I'm thrilled as hell to be going home to my brothers, but my heart is breaking at the same time.

I don't even know what his last name is. That's one of the first things I intend to find out. Maybe I'll be able to ease his pain and my heart by showing him we were not responsible for whatever he thinks we did.

I snuggle back into him more, loving the feeling of

his chest against my back and his breath on my neck. I just want to go to sleep and wake up in his arms.

I lay like that for almost an hour, him close to me with my hand wrapped around his in front of our bodies. Maxim suddenly rolls over on his back, his hand moves above his head covering his eyes, now's the time.

I ease myself off the bed, barely making any movement and then tip-toe over to the closet. I shut the door quietly, so I can turn on the light.

I almost moan loudly, relieved when I see all my clothes packed inside my bag. I hurry up and take those out. First things first, I've got to get him secured to the bed so I can get away.

At the bottom of my bag is a Fail-Safe. This looks just like a regular gym bag, but this bottom part was added for us by the guy we buy these from. It makes it a lot easier to transfer guns and equipment this way.

Finding the almost invisible hidden zipper, I open it up. I can see four of my knives and three sets of hand-cuffs. I'm starting to feel giddy all over.

I silently take two pairs of handcuffs out, making sure the fuckers don't clink together. That would be all I need now is to get caught when I'm so close.

Turning off the light, I make my way back over to Maxim who hasn't moved an inch. I'm going to have to be fast about this.

As quietly as I can, I click one pair of handcuffs to the wooden bed frame on the right side of him and then I do the left side with the other pair. This is where it gets tricky, his right arm is the one that's above his head, that's the one I'm going to have to get first.

I stand next to him on the side of the bed, quickly grabbing his hand yanking it back securing the cuff around it. I don't wait I scramble over him on the bed, it's faster than actually walking around. But this could be more dangerous because he has a way to grab a hold of me, but since he's been sleeping, he'll be out of it.

Maxim's eyes open in confusion and it takes a few seconds for him to realize what's going on, but by the time he comes to, I've already grabbed his left hand and just finished attaching it to the cuffs.

"What the fuck are you doing Anna? You won't get away with this." He tells me as I start to walk back towards the closet.

I turn back and wink at him, "yes I will."

CHAPTER 25

*A*nna
It feels so good to finally be in my own clothes again. I'm standing in Maxim's closet and I just finished putting on my black cargo pants and my Henley sweatshirt. I was very fortunate that they brought my combat boots, I was going to have to go barefoot.

I have three knives on me one strapped on my inner thigh. Like Laura Croft, but instead of guns, I prefer knives. The other two are in my boots.

I walked back in and look at a furious Maxim still handcuffed to the bed. They're little rings around his wrists where he must have been trying to break free.

He just looks at my changed appearance in shock and fascination. He must have not gone through my bag to see what was in there, dumbass.

"Would you have let me go?"

"No," he answers truthfully.

"Would you have killed my brothers?"

"Yes," the same truthful answer comes from him.

"That's why I have to go. I wish you would tell me what was going on, why you are so hell-bent on revenge."

I know I shouldn't, but I lay down next to him, putting my head on his chest. "I wish things could have been different."

"Me too," he says solemnly.

I kiss him on the mouth, then I get off the bed. I noticed he had a phone charger earlier. I quickly grab that and bind his legs together, then tie them to the edge of the footboard. I need to make sure that he doesn't thrash making too much noise.

Maxim hasn't said anything about his legs being tied up he's just watching me calculating and thinking.

I walk over to him give him one more glorious kiss, which he returns just as frantically. When we break away, Maxim says with a deep intimidating voice, "you're mine Anna, I will come for you."

"I know." I almost feel the same way, but this can never be. A lone tear makes its way down, falling on the pillow next to his head. I quickly stuff the under-wear from last night into his mouth.

I need at least ten minutes to get out of here. I worked my hair back into a ponytail as I walked over to his desk, I need his keys and the card that lets you get into every room instead of using a code, faster.

I don't dare look back as I use the card and make my way to the hallway. If I do, I'm afraid I won't go.

Once outside, the door shuts and secures behind me I take in deep cleansing breaths and count out one, two, three then repeat. I need to get into my head. This is now a case I'm working on and the person I'm going to be saving is me and my brothers.

I wish Maxim had a cell phone, but he didn't, so I left empty-handed. I'm in another wing of the house. I still need to walk down a long hallway with multiple doors. I curse myself for a second, I should have taken his whole wallet-he might've had his ID in it. I still don't know who this man is.

I could go back but that's valuable time wasted. I walk with my guard up, listening and surveying my surroundings, waiting for an attack at any time. Most of the guards will be shocked to see me like this and their confusion will pay off.

I reach the stairs that connect to the ones leading up to my room. Once you go down at the bottom, you're in a grand foyer and you could take two different staircases. I listen, hearing mumbled voices coming from somewhere downstairs. I need to make my way to the garage.

A door opens behind me. Shit, this is too fast, at least it's only one man. Fuck, it's Troy, he's the one that tried to manhandle me a week ago outside.

I quickly put my hands down, kind of holding them

between my legs. I'm hoping to block the visibility of the knife.

"Well, well, look who it is." He sneers at me. I know this man doesn't like me, he's a fucking douche.

"Please don't hurt me or tell Maxim. I was just going downstairs to get something to eat. It will only take a minute and I'll be right back in my room." I painfully plead. This shit is getting old fast.

The man laughs, "even better, no one knows you're out here. I think you should follow me back to my room." He comes over and grabs me by the back of my head, yanking my ponytail in the direction of the room he just vacated.

I use the palm of my hand, quickly jabbing him in the sternum. I've had that done to me, it hurts like a bitch. My knee is positioned perfectly in line with his balls. I didn't need to do that move, but I made me feel hella good. While he's still standing up, I kick straight into his kneecap, that move drops his ass on the floor. He'll be hurting for a while.

His mouth is opened but there's too much pain for him to speak. He's probably wondering who the fuck I am.

I kneel down beside him quickly, I don't want to take too much time, but I can't let this moment pass. "One day I'm going to visit you and it's just going to be us. I'll make you pay for everything you've done to me and probably every other innocent woman you've messed with. Remember my name bitch."

I quickly go down the steps, that guy is a pussy, so it'll take longer for him to get up. Now I only have several minutes before I need to get out of here.

I have to walk towards the back of the house to get to the garage area. Why couldn't it be right by the foyer? Where most houses have theirs.

As I come around the corner, one of the guards almost runs right into me. I've seen this one a couple of times but not too much. He's a young one probably newly recruited.

I don't even give him a chance to say anything or to make a move. I punch him right in the throat and let him fall to his knees. I'm not a total bitch, I explain to him, "don't gasp for breath and take shallow slow ones, you'll be fine in no time."

I can see the garage door from where I'm standing, it's actually right next to the pantry door in the kitchen. I'm almost there.

It opens as Booker comes in swinging his car keys around his index finger, not a care in the world. I think he was actually humming. He hasn't noticed me yet. My hands drop instantly again trying to block my knife.

I can't really say that I've become friends with one of the men that helped kidnap me, but I've become closer to him than everybody else. Underneath the deadly exterior, he's a really good guy and very loyal. But his loyalty doesn't lie with me.

Booker spots me as he's walking and halts,

wondering what I'm doing here and probably why I'm dressed like this.

"Hey baby girl, what are you doing down here?" He stares at me trying to figure out what's going on, titling his bald and shiny head to the side.

"I was going to make something to eat for me and Maxim. He sleeps like a rock." A chuckle from me escapes trying to lighten the mood.

Booker smiles, "yeah he does. There's a bunch of pre-made food in the fridge already, but you should come over to the sitting room. We're having our weekly game night. I bet you can give most of these guys a run for their money."

"Maybe," I laugh really awkwardly and start to look around for a weapon. Time is running out and I've got to get out of here before those two other guys are found.

On the stove two feet away from me is a cast iron skillet. Now that will definitely take down Booker. One of the knives I have will do the job, too, but I just can't, the man's been the only one that's been kind to me.

Booker walks past me and straight to the fridge, his back is to me as he starts going through the contents, reading off some of the stuff that's in there that we might want to eat.

I put my head down to focus feeling horrible for what I'm about to do, then I grab the pan in my hand, and I tell him "I'm sorry."

He says "what," as he turns around and that's when I

smack him right in the side of the head. He goes down like a lump of bricks, not even moving.

I curse under my breath and bend down and check that he's okay. His breathing and his pulse are fine. Opening the freezer, I grab one of the ice packs that are in there and lay it gently on the side of his face that I hit. Even though he's out cold, this should help with swelling.

The keys that he was twirling in his hand has a fob on them. I snatch them up quickly and head to the garage. I cursed myself earlier for not grabbing Maxim's phone, I realized I left my bag upstairs, but there's not much left in it.

Using the unlock button I make my way over to a brand-new Maserati that beeped. Well, at least I'll be going home in style.

Pushing the button on the visor to open the garage door, I want to just peel out and race away, that shouldn't draw attention to me, yeah right. At least the windows are tinted, nobody knows who I am.

I drive casually down to the gate, the guardsman on duty there lets me out giving me a brief nod as I make my way into the night.

After three weeks I'm free and I'm going home to my brothers.

CHAPTER 26

*M*axim
    I yank on the handcuffs trying to at least break the bedpost to no avail. I'm one strong mother-fucker and so is my furniture. "FUCK," I scream spitting out the wadded panties in my mouth. Hoping someone can hear me.

It's the guards weekly poker game that lasts from night till morning. It shouldn't be long, though, somebody had to notice Anna escaping. Or maybe I need to hire a whole new fucking staff.

Who the fuck is this woman?

She's been playing us the whole time. She's highly trained, most likely from her brothers and her father. She made all of us think that she was weak, just waiting for the right moment to make her move.

God, if that doesn't fucking turn me on. I'm already starting to get hard again. All I can think about is naked sparing with her, I bet she's good. I've seen her brother's fight, and they are insanely good. Not better than me, though. I was fascinated with her before, but now I'm enthralled.

I will get her back and she will be mine. Eventually, she will come to understand my revenge and the demise of her family.

It is time for me to get to the bottom of everything she's mentioned, a stalker, and a mole on the inside. Maybe this isn't the fault of the Moretti's after all. No, I shake my head, it was their fault. I've been gunning for them for months. Even if there was someone inside messing up their cases, it's their fault for not handling it. I will hold everyone accountable.

I yank on my legs trying to get them free, again. Maybe if I can break apart this bed, I can get out of here. I keep yanking and pulling, I can feel my muscles straining. I'm a big guy and I can't even budge my fucking feet. God, is this a double Boy Scout knot or some shit? *She's good.*

The door to my room bursts open and a beaten looking Booker comes running to my side.

"Who the fuck is that girl? She took me out with a cast iron skillet, then when I was unconscious, she put an ice bag on my head, for fucking swelling."

I start to laugh at Booker as he huffs mad that somebody got the better hand. "That's what I'm trying to figure out man. Do you think you could get me out of this?"

He nods, then quickly goes out the way he came in. Wow, she even took out Booker, no one has ever done that. Even guys high up in the mob, I'm talking fuckers compared to *Scarface* and *Gotti*. Those guys can't even touch this huge motherfucker.

Booker comes running back in, with him he has two of my lower-level guys. One of them has metal cutters in his hands.

Neither one of them can keep their shocked expressions off their face seeing me in this position. I snap at them, "hurry the fuck up."

Booker watches in amusement as the handcuff chains are snapped apart. I look at my lower level guys and snap out orders, "run down to the garage and see what car is missing. Put an APB out on it. I want several guys going after her, she cannot get away."

The men run out of the room following orders. I quickly jump into my clothes, wishing that I had the damn key to remove the rest of the handcuffs on both of my wrists.

Booker follows me as I make my way down to my office. I need to find out what this girl did. As we pass the kitchen, I can see Troy and another one of my lower-level guys sitting at the kitchen table while my in-house-attendant Martha is helping them.

Troy looks beaten to shit and the other guy just has a mark on his neck but is breathing deeply. Troy has an ice pack on his balls and one on his elevated knee. Booker notices the same thing I do and starts to laugh.

They look at me but don't say anything. They can tell I'm in a rush, and probably notice the metal on my wrists. Both of us quickly walk by. I wait for Booker to open up my office since I no longer have my key and I don't want to punch in the numbers.

Sitting behind my desk, it takes several minutes for the system to load up and for me to rewind the security footage inside the house.

Booker and I watch with open mouths as Anna stealthily makes her way to the garage. Taking out Troy like a professional, and not giving the other guy even a chance to react, just putting him down.

We could see her amicability when she runs into Booker, she doesn't want to hurt him. We both cringe as the skillet hits his face. I can hear Booker sigh next to me when he sees that he's out cold and she opens the freezer and puts an ice pack on his face.

Anna quickly grabs his fob, which I now know is for the Maserati, he was bringing it back, and she takes off.

"She is our number one priority, we need to find her." I say to Booker; his face is starting to swell up, making his left eye pinch closed. "This comes before anything else, I want everybody pulled onto this right now. Anna is mine and I want her back."

Booker quickly turns and heads out the door. He needs to start pulling teams together.

I'm coming to get you, baby.

CHAPTER 27

*a*nna
     I slam the steering wheel of the expensive car with my right hand and scream, "YES, YES, YES," to no one in particular.

The euphoric taste of freedom is heavenly bliss. I feel giddy and excited as I drive along the New York highways.

Now I need to figure out where I'm going, since Maxim and his men have told me my not-so-secret apartment has been found out.

That only leaves the safe house in Brooklyn. The Moretti's have had this forever and only the five of us know about it. So, unless one of my brothers are the traitor, then I should be fine.

That's the only option I have right now. I don't have anything with me, no phone, no money, nothing. They might be waiting for me at one of my brother's places, I don't want to take a chance of getting caught again right now.

I've had mixed emotions ever since I left. A part of me still wants to be back at the house with Maxim and Booker, but the rational side of my brain tells me this isn't right.

I need to get word to my brothers. I need to make sure that they're safe and that no harm comes to them. Maxim never said he was done with his revenge with them, and I have a feeling he isn't.

I don't know what I would do if anything ever happened to them, especially if I had a chance to stop it. All of them need to be warned, then we can figure out a plan together.

I also need to figure out Maxim. What is his connection with my family? I don't have enough fingers and toes to count the number of times I've asked myself the same question.

It's also time to find my stalker. Time to put an end to this creep. I just hope when I tell my brother's about him, or I guess it could be her, they don't go ballistic on me.

I grip the steering wheel harder, for some reason I feel more stressed now than when I was back at my kidnappers' house. It's most likely because I have a chance to actually make sense of everything, even though it'll take some work. Maybe I can right some wrongs.

Nobody likes having a million questions with no answers, ever.

I look at the time on the clock it reads five a.m. It's pitch black outside and creepy as fuck. It seems whenever you go into the worst part of town, the nights are darker, and the weather is colder.

I know there's a chop shop several blocks away from the safe house that's run by a small-time gang. They may be small time, but I believe they make a shit ton of money when they get the right cars. I can see them drooling over this Maserati.

Unless Maxim is a total and complete idiot, he's got to have GPS tracking on this car. I don't know how to disable it or where it would be located. I've heard of overly obsessed people putting more than one in their cars. I can see him doing that in this and his other ones.

I park on the side of a deserted road across from the white desolate looking warehouse. It's not as big as your average ones, but big enough that it still looks creepy as hell.

Several men are outside they just watch me as I park. I doubt if they've ever had a car brought straight to them. One of the men motions for a guy to go inside most likely to get others.

I start taking deep breaths. Defeating multiple men here won't be too hard, because most of them aren't trained and well-practiced. They're usually really drunk or high from what I've seen.

Tonight though, I just don't have it in me. I just

want to shower and sleep. I make my breathing go deeper. I can't even let them see the trace of fear that I have, they'll eat that shit up.

I count seven men walking towards me. All different shapes and sizes from lanky to fat. Only a couple of them look like they actually take care of themselves. And one of them is in the middle, leading the pack. He's got to be the one in charge, I'll keep my focus on him.

I step out of my car, lightly running my hand over my knife that's strapped to my thigh, just checking. If I'm going to need it, it's going to be now.

I stand right in front of the car with my legs spread slightly in a fighting stance. I'm not going to take any chances.

They all walk up in front of me, forming a half-moon. The guy who I believe is the leader starts to talk. "Well, what do we have here?" He looks me up and down taking in my features, then finally settle on my knives.

Smart man. I don't say anything, I just wait to see how this is all going to play out. It would be nice if one time the guys come up to me and say, "Ma'am, what can we help you with?" It always has to be a show of dominance of whose balls are bigger.

I proved myself right as the one on the far left starts to inch his way closer to me. It's freezing out here, it's got to be the beginning of February. I don't even know the freaking date right now. This idiot is wearing a wife beater and a pair of jean shorts.

The fifty to seventy-five lbs. of extra weight on him is probably keeping him insulated. He moves to grab me by the back of the neck. On instinct, I have my knife out and press right between his legs.

"You have two choices you fat fucker. I can either cut your artery one inch to the right or I can take off the tip of your dick one inch to the left, decide." He gasps in shock. I know he wasn't expecting that. That's about the only enjoyment I get doing the same shit anymore.

The leader, one of the healthier looking men, bends over holding his stomach and howls out laughing. "Damn girl, let him go. Ain't nothing going to happen to you." He barely gasps out.

I re-sheath my knife and push the guy back towards the position he came from, so I look at the man that seems to be in charge. "I need to get rid of this car."

"Baby, you definitely came to the right place," he starts to walk towards me. I hold out my hand to stop him. I don't need anyone in my personal space. Being a New Yorker, I should realize I no longer have personal space.

He stops instantly and just interlocks his fingers behind his back. And nods for me to continue.

"You don't want the man and his guys that own this car to find you. I hope you guys work fast. I don't know shit about GPS, all I know is that they're looking for the car and me."

The guy nods, this definitely isn't their first rodeo. I toss the car keys to him, which he catches without a problem. None of the other men made a sound, they just keep watching me with their gleaming eyes, free money. The other guy that decided to get to close is grunting like he wishes everyone could turn around just for a second so he could finish what he started. I give him a smile while winking.

One of the men, really thin and lanky, asks, "where are you heading to?"

"I have a place not far from here." I look at him as I answer.

The leader chimes in, "I'll have two of my men follow you to make sure you get there safely."

I shake my head, "if your men follow me, I'm going to cut them, and they won't be returning."

"Damn, they won't follow you, but this isn't the best neighborhood, even for someone who seems to know what they're doing." He tries to reason with me.

"I understand," I say over my shoulder walking in the direction of the apartment. "Time is money and so are your lives, don't get caught with this car."

Several of the men nod as the leader looks directly at me. The rest of the guys grab the keys to pull the car inside the garage.

"I like you," I pause and turn around. "If you ever

get bored or looking for something different, come back and find me."

He's actually really sincere and sweet with that statement. I smile, then take off in a slight jog. I don't want to be stuck out here just in case Maxim and his guys find that car.

I make it to the apartment, which is five blocks away in under ten minutes. The nice thing about this place is that there are no keys used, only codes like they were at my captors' house.

All the different siblings have their own code and we don't know each other's. We're the only ones that know about this place. We never visit, it's just in case of emergencies for us if something ever bad happens on a job.

Jax will be able to see what person entered the apartment. I don't even believe that there's a phone line in here. I'm not sure, hopefully there's just food. I haven't been here in several years.

The cleaning service they hired come out once a month. I think they replace nonperishables after a certain amount of time, but perishables are never stocked.

I reach the building and of course, we don't have a key for entry. There's no doorman but there are multiple apartments to buzz. I hit every single apartment except for the managers.

To be honest, I felt guilty, it's only five a.m. not that

many people are up at this time. I do receive a fuck you and several what the fucks.

But just like I hoped, eventually somebody buzzes me in. I could have sat here and waited for somebody to walk out. I'd probably have to sit here for two hours out in the open and I could be retaken at any time.

Maxim did promise me that I am his and he is coming for me. That alone gives me chills. I miss him, I just can't help it. We had such a great connection and he was my first sexual experience, but family and my brothers come first. Their lives mean the world to me.

I take the stairs up to the fourth floor, then enter my code. 3 3 1 6.

I did try to use all fours or threes, but Jax wouldn't have it, so we finally settled on this. Well, I blurted out the first number I could think of. Jax knows all of our codes, he is the one who set everything up.

The apartment is just how I remembered, the buildings a decent building. It's not too dilapidated and it's not for the rich.

A lot of families and businessmen live here. The two-bedroom is very bland, not even a touch of a home. I walk around and everything looks immaculately clean, so the cleaning service is still coming.

In the living room are just your basic brown leather couches with an average size flat screen TV. The kitchen is stocked with non-perishables, *thankfully*.

I grab a bottle of water and head down to one of the

rooms to find some clothes. I need a shower and a very long ass nap, maybe I'll sleep for a week or a month.

It doesn't take long before I'm showered and changed. I settle in the small guest room. I always feel awkward using the bigger one even though no one really owns it, it feels like it's not my house.

It takes less than five minutes before I'm out cold, and I never did check to see if there was a landline.

CHAPTER 28

*a*nna
My name keeps dancing and floating inside my head, all garbled. I keep trying to reach it but it's like a puzzle piece that can't be solved.

The blankets are ripped from the bed, causing my eyes to pop open and a gasp to escape from my mouth. I'm lifted up before I can even get my bearings, a scream escapes from my mouth. *Where are my knives?*

I can hear chuckling as I'm pulled tightly into a bear hug. "What the hell! Let me down," I scream.

I push away from my intruder and look at him in the eyes. "Colt, you son of a bitch, you scared the shit out of me."

He starts to laugh then pulls me in for another tight hug. "You scared the shit out of us little sis. We have never been more worried. No one had a clue what the hell happened to you."

I wrap my arms around him and hug him back as tight as I can and let the tears just flow. I never thought I would see them again.

Colt starts to rub up and down my arms. "Come on, lets head to the living room." I look down to make sure I'm dressed, that would have been awkward.

I have on a pair of green leggings and a black tank-top. I quickly grab one of my big oversized sweaters and throw it on. I don't even need shoes or socks, I cranked the heater up in this bitch when I got here.

Wiping the tears from my eyes, I follow Colt out to the living area. I'm really glad he's here, he's my favorite. The one I'm the closest with.

As soon as Colt's huge frame moves out of the way as he heads towards the kitchen, I stop dead in my tracks. Sitting on the couch are my other three brothers, Jax, Mason and Finn each drinking a beer.

Isn't it morning? I quickly glance towards the clock on the wall, it shows that it's two p.m. Well I did go to bed kind of late or early.

Finn and Mason both stand up at the same time and move towards me. Jax just watches me like he's trying to figure out what happened instead of actually asking.

Mason is my brother that I'm least connected with, he's not involved in the family business that much. He's still my brother and I still love him. He wraps me in a big hug and then moves out of the way for Finn.

Finn starts to look me up and down like a guy

might do to a woman in a club, but he's doing it as a doctor, not a potential fun night.

I hold up my hand before he can even say anything. "There's nothing wrong with me. I wasn't hurt or injured in any way. I'm totally fine."

"Are you sure? I can check you really fast just to be on the safe side." Finn looks at me with pleading eyes. I know he wants to just make sure.

"I swear, I was locked in a room, that's about the extent of everything." He nods letting this go for now. I know he'll be back later, or he'll watch me like a hawk.

Finn gives me a hug then both him and Mason walk back to the couch to sit down. Jax comes up and pulls me into a fatherly hug.

"I want to know everything. Whoever did this to you is going to fucking pay, it's been almost three weeks," he seethes.

"I know." I'm just so happy to see all of them. Jax holds me tighter, breaking the dam I managed to keep in place. I sob uncontrollably, it feels like a howl from deep inside is escaping. I'm not just crying from my ordeal, I'm crying because I could've lost my brothers.

"I never thought I'd see you guys again," I choke out. Jax moves me over to the recliner and sits back down on the couch with Mason and Finn.

Colts sits on the floor right across from me, they're all watching me. I got a lot to tell them, but damn I need coffee first. Colt must have been reading my mind because in his hand is a cup as he leans forward onto his knees and hands it to me.

"Thank you," I mutter. "I guess I should just start at the beginning. I was taken three weeks ago, I believe it's three weeks, I'm not sure of the date, by my new neighbor at the cabin."

Colt and Jax share look, they came to visit me at the cabin. I'm not sure if they saw the neighbor or not.

"I don't know who he is, all I know is that his first name is Maxim and for some reason, he wants all of us dead. A couple of weeks ago," I take a sip of my coffee hoping to calm my nerves a little bit, then a few more sips before I continue. "Maxim had guards ready to take all of you out. I had to beg and plead for your lives, at least to buy myself more time."

All of their expressions remain stoic, they just watch and wait for me to continue. I don't give them any more information on exactly what I had to do to save them, it's none of their business.

"This guy has to be a higher upper for one of the families. I'm pretty sure that we did a job for him or one of his loved ones that went wrong. He kept saying it was our fault that she's dead."

Jax's eyebrows start to clinch together. I can tell he's thinking, running over the possible jobs that we have done that ended badly.

It's kind of stressing me out, I don't want to be the center of attention. I wish somebody would say something. I decide to keep sipping my coffee and be quiet.

Mason chimes in, "what does Maxim look like?"

I described him in great detail to my brothers, not leaving anything out. It's like I'm reminiscing just for myself.

I look at all of them as I speak, "I had to get back to you guys. I had to make sure you were safe and that you know what might still be coming."

Colt gets up to from the floor and grabs my coffee cup. He heads into the kitchen and refills it, then grabs four more beers.

They must have bought the alcohol with them. That shit wasn't here last night.

That reminds me, "how did you guys know I was here?"

Jax gives me his trademark smirk, "I like to run the logs several times a day for all of our properties, and that's when I noticed your code hit on this place. I called everybody and we met over here."

I nodded, I figured that would happen, "this was the only place I could think of. I had no phone, no money and I stole the guys Maserati. We should really get a landline here."

Mason, loving the expensive cars, looks at me, "Maserati?"

"I left it at the chop shop several blocks to the east." They all start laughing except for Mason, I think this actually hurts his heart.

"There's a couple more things I need to talk to you guys about. Someone named Cruz came to the house, I think he's in charge of the Mexican Mafia. I'm not really sure, I haven't dealt much with them. Anyway, he and his guys broke into Maxim's place. They were there for me, there's a five-million-dollar bounty on my head.

I expected what happened to happen. All of my brothers, except for Jax instantly stood up and screamed, "what."

I hold up my hands, "I have no clue who did it at all. Cruz wouldn't tell me anything. He just said I was his meal ticket. And I know it had to be high for them to hit a place like Maxim's."

Jax looks at me and asks, "can you find his place again?"

"I'm not sure, I don't think so. I was really high on adrenaline and had been driving for over two hours to get here. Hopefully, one day it will come back to me."

He nods, "we'll come back to that later, after you have a chance to rest and get your mind clear." Jax stands up, "you don't have much here, I want you to come stay at the main house with me."

I was thinking about how to say no to him, but I didn't get a chance when Colt pipes in, "that's an excellent idea, I'll go with you we can hang out like we used to."

He actually looks sincere and worried. "What, you want me to be your wing woman and help you get laid?" We all bust out laughing.

Jax starts to walk towards the door. "Let's go, I don't

know how secure this place is, or this area is anymore. I don't want to stay longer than needed."

I don't move, I stay seated as all my brothers casually head towards the door. I can't put this off any longer. I've been missing for so long I don't think they'll hurt me now.

"I need you guys to sit down, there still one more thing." They all look back at me and then slowly take their spots. Colt doesn't sit on the floor, he just sits on the arm of my chair.

The best thing I could do is just blurt it out and get it over with. "Over a year ago, I started getting packages from a stalker."

I wait for the explosions to come but it never happens. Jax and Mason look pissed, while Colt and Finn seem really worried.

I continue with my story. I tell them every package I can think of, including the roses, photos and lingerie. The lingerie one was hard to tell my brothers. "I'm not sure what the last package was because Maxim never told me."

I told them that I stored it all with the original card and a picture of the gift at my apartment, but it was broken into and the stuff is gone. I don't have my cell phone right now. Everything was saved on the cloud, so when we get to Jax's house I can bring it all up.

I wait quietly, I spent at least thirty minutes telling them about the stalker and nobody has said a word.

Jax gets up and heads out the front door. They're

pissed. Finn looks at me with sad eyes and then follows.

I stand up when Colt stands, he puts his arm around me, and we walk out together. I'm relieved that it's off my chest but I know that this conversation isn't done.

I still have to deal with my brothers before I can figure out who Maxim and my stalker is.

CHAPTER 29

*M*axim

Anna has only been gone since yesterday and I feel like I'm going out of my fucking head. I can't think straight and can't sleep. All I want is her back to my house and in my bed with me.

I let myself down in a big way not looking into how heavily trained she was. I got to admit, it was hot as hell, but still, that's not my style. She could have killed me if she wanted to.

I just can't wait to get my hands on her. God, my dick is starting to get hard again just thinking about her. I've got to find her and bring her back, whether she wants it or not.

I think it actually shocked all the men, we were expecting this little sweet innocent naive girl, even though she was a Moretti with four older brothers. She did have some sass in her mouth, but who wouldn't.

We sure as hell didn't expect she was a trained killer. Even Booker is in awe. I know if I didn't have my sights on her, he would definitely be making a move. That kind of woman is one in a million.

Damn, I get up from my desk and head over to my decanter. I don't even try to be gentle, I just fill the damn glass to the top and slam the whole thing back. At the rate I'm going, I'll just start drinking straight from the bottle.

Early this morning, I had a bunch of my men go over to the cabin I was in and wipe it clean. No fingerprints, no DNA. No one will ever be able to find out who owned it. I've gone through at least a hundred shell companies. It would take years to trace it back to me and that's only if they're good.

I had a few of them sneak into the Moretti cabin and clean that up, too, just places that I've been. I also wanted them to do a sweep to see if they've found any more of the stalker stuff. But there was nothing, it was all gone, most likely sent to her new place.

Booker printed me out every single picture of all the items the stalker sent and the cards. He and a couple of other men have started to piece the puzzle together by visiting the florists and delivery places.

Everything was done using a prepaid Visa. They never met the person who wanted the stuff delivered, they believed it was a man, probably in his late twenties or early thirties based on his voice. He had no accent, so this leaves us at another dead end.

There's got to be a link, a missing piece somewhere. I sit back down at my desk right as Booker walks in.

He slumps in the chair across from me, he looks just as exhausted as I do. We both want to find our girl.

"Anything," I ask, taking another drink.

He shakes his head, "nothing really useful. We did find the location the Maserati was at last. She conveniently parked it right across the street from a chop shop."

I start to laugh and then Booker joins in, "smart girl," I mutter.

I'm going to miss that car but not more than her. I make a note to myself to call the insurance-company later. I also need to report it stolen.

"You know," Booker starts, here we go again. "Maybe now you could just try to get the girl and leave the family alone. Decide what's more important. Work on the case with her. Let her know that you're going to leave the brothers alone, as long as she helps you with the case. You both can figure this out together."

"Nope, not going to happen. They need to be held accountable. That's still my first priority." Booker shakes his head.

I can't let this go. My sister, an innocent girl, lost her life. The Moretti's fucked up, they need to pay for this. We've already taken care of the Cooper guy, but anyone else involved needs to pay the price. This is my family legacy. This is how we've done things for years.

"Look man, I don't want to argue with you." Booker

says as he stands, "but this damn revenge thing is going to ruin everything, *everything*."

I'm not in the mood to listen to this shit again. I love the man like my own brother, but it's been a constant argument for the past two weeks.

"This will cause a war between your family and theirs. Look man, I can tell you have feelings for the girl. Who do you think she's going to side with? If you could just open your mind and not be so dead set on making sure that everybody's dead, maybe you guys could actually figure it out. Who's the mole? That's what you need to do man."

He doesn't even wait for a response, he just leaves the room and shuts the door behind him.

I know he has a point but I'm not sure I'm going to be able to let this rage simmer down, it's been boiling for over several months now. It's the Ivanov way. We do not take shit from anyone, we definitely do not stand down. It's going to make me look weak. I didn't get this high up by being a pussy.

Anna will come around, maybe I don't have to take out all of her brothers, just the ones that had a finger in this. It will take time to figure out who exactly, but I know she'll eventually help me.

Even if I have to, I'll keep her locked up with me. I don't want to lose her a second time. It might take years for her to love me. I've never said this about anybody, but I can see this woman as my wife and the mother of my children.

Of course, I want somebody to be here of their own free will, voluntarily in love with me, but if I can't have that, I'll just take it. I know she'll come around, she has to.

I'm not going to let her get away again and I sure as shit ain't going to let anybody else have her, especially this little stalker fuck. I'm going to end him.

I hope you're ready babe. Very soon I'm coming for you. I smile and slam back my second drink. God, I'm going to turn into a fucking alcoholic.

CHAPTER 30

*a*nna
Forty years ago, my parents received the deal of a lifetime. A very popular rock band back then owned a brownstone right by Central Park.

Always being high and drunk made them the owners of a dilapidated house. The lead singer needed to offload the property and fast, he decided never to pay taxes his whole career.

My father was able to pick up the brownstone for only five million dollars. That one is worth seventeen million today.

Of course, they had to rip out the carpet and remodel the whole damn thing. Basically, tear it down to the skeleton and start from scratch, but it was totally worth it, it's gorgeous.

Over the years after they kept popping out the kids, they decided to add to it. The elderly woman on the right passed away. Her family that was located in Ireland had no inclination-to come and live in the United States, so they sold that brownstone to my parents for eight million.

About five years later the house on the left had sat empty for a good twenty years or so. No one knows the story with that one. My dad was able to get it from a tax sale for four and half million.

It took a lot of money, sweat and tears to connect the three units and update them all the same way.

There's a total of eighteen bedrooms with six floors. Let's not forget the twenty-three bathrooms. I love this place, it reminds me of my childhood.

My childhood home is full of all the original hardwood floors. When they removed the carpet, cherry hardwood floors laid underneath in perfect condition, all they needed was to be was cleaned and shined. The kitchens, all three of have been updated with stainless steel appliances. The one in the main house is the masterpiece.

The house to the left is partially used for the guards and the one in the right side is partially used for the help.

Marble floors lay throughout, the same color scheme in the kitchen, bathrooms and dining room. Every other place has hardwood floors. The details aren't as exquisite as the Mountainside cabin but they're still just as gorgeous.

When I was younger, I decided on one of the attic

rooms. I love that space up there. I don't even think you can call it legally a bedroom, but it spans half of the entire area of the main house.

The place has family pictures throughout. There are so many hallways with pictures I can see my mom anytime I want to. The master bedroom was left alone. Keeping it that way for my father whenever he comes back, and it has all my mom's stuff in there, like her makeup and perfume even though it's been eleven years.

Being back here is driving me crazy. Only Colt and Jax are staying here all the time but every now and then, Finn and Mason show up. My brothers hover over me as my parents did.

There are three offices located in this house. Jax has been letting me use the main office, it has the most research equipment.

My family has deals with the DEA, CIA, FBI and etcetera. We legally can get on their databases. Yes, they do track what we do and what we search for, but we need this information to move ahead with a lot of our cases. Thankfully our best researcher is Mason's better half, Lee. She's working just as hard as the rest of us. It's frustrating for everyone else, because I'm the only one who has seen my kidnappers.

Jax and Colt have grabbed the files from all of our cases in the last year. I think we only needed to go back about six months at most, but we wanted to be certain.

I've been here for over three weeks now and I'm

going freaking insane. I started with the farthest case back and went through it meticulously in detail with every photo in every file.

I even had a magnifying glass for family pictures that had others in the background. If nothing helped from our files, then I would start my internet research on all the different databases. I needed to check every single family member out, even if they were extended.

Colt has been in here helping me like crazy, which is awesome. He would scan the paperwork in the files for the name Maxim or Booker. I even gave him Troy and some of the other guard names that I heard.

While he would do this, I would look through all the pictures and their captions. This process cut down my time in half.

We both worked tirelessly, almost twelve hours a day, we're now on the Sophia case. The last case I was on before everything went to shit. I've only been on one case after that, Johnny's.

I really need to call Monica to see how they're doing. I make a mental note to myself.

The tears are coming heavily as I expected them to when I open up the file on Sofia. I relive that night in my mind almost every day but now I'm seeing it in pictures and words.

This case will take half of the day or most of it because of my emotional state and the huge family that Sophia has being in the Russian mafia.

Colt wasn't able to be here today, they had

another job that they had to do. So, I spent the first two hours going through the thick and heavy files just looking at the names and a few pictures that we had attached to the papers. They were all of Sophia, no one else.

Dima Ivanov is the younger brother that originally contracted us for this job. Really nice man, several years older than me, he's twenty-eight. Well, I've heard differently, but he was very nice to me.

I start pulling up the databases. I've gone through the FBI and Homeland Security and then I go over to the CIA that's when the shit hits the fan.

There are multiple files and pictures on this family, but it doesn't take me long to stumble across a dark and gorgeous man with light eyes, his arms around Sophia. It looks like they're at a picnic or a family gathering.

They're not the only ones in the picture, the man also has his arm around another woman while Dima is on the other side of Sophia.

The tears are flowing freely now as I realize that strange man is Maxim, and he's the elusive head of the Russian mafia. *Fuck.* I always knew their older brother was in hiding. I just never realized it was him.

I quickly start to print out several copies of this picture. I need to get this to Jax right away. This is so much bigger than we thought it would be.

This isn't a small little family problem, this is a huge fucking problem and now I believe more than anything that Maxim will hold true to his word about killing the men in my life.

This man has connections that some of us can only dream of, he could just say one word and countries would crumble.

With his power, he probably hasn't gotten rid of my brothers, as a favor to me but only time will tell. I left him. Holy shit, I handcuffed the man to a bedpost and stole his Maserati.

If you look at it from my side, it was totally legit. I did it to save my life and the lives of my brothers. But if you look at it from the mafia side, it was an act of betrayal. God, we are so fucked.

I start to shake as I grab the copies and Sophia's file. I heard the boys come back earlier, so I know their job is done, which means that they're just having a conclusion meeting in one of the other offices.

It doesn't take me long to find them. I can hear them laughing, using the office on the guard side. It's got a conference room attached to it unlike the other two, but the office is a lot smaller.

I don't even knock, all of us like our privacy especially when a door is closed but I can't wait.

Jax immediately stands up from his place at the head of the table when he sees my face. I can see Colt and Finn seated but no Mason. I imagine he went back to work for the day.

Four of our new hire guards are in there, too, Jax spits out for them to leave. Colt and Finn don't move, they just watch me as Jax comes around and locks the conference room door, then looks at me. "You found him?"

I nod, stumbling over to the table. I want to give the guys each a picture, so they understand what we're dealing with. Sophia was my case, so they might not have seen the pictures. I'm not sure if they know who she is but I know that they know who Dima is, and they've heard of his ruthless brother.

I put Sophia's case on the table that has Sofia Ivanov in big letters on the front of it.

It clicks for Jax almost instantly as he mutters, "fuck." He shakes his head and looks up at the ceiling, his jaw starts to clench. He's just as worried as I am. He reaches out his hand and gives mine a squeeze of reassurance.

It takes Colt and Finn a few more seconds to put the pieces together. Finn looks at me and points at Maxim, "is this him?" I nod.

Jax looks over to Colt. "I need you to call an emergency meeting, now. I want only the heads of all of the families, they can bring their sergeant in arms if they need to."

Colt gives me a kiss on the head as he runs out of the room. Jax looks over at Finn. "I need you to call Mason and get him here right away, explain what's happening. It would be safer if we all stayed together in this house for a while, including Lee."

Jax looks at Finn, "I also want us to get more

guards, but I'll have Mason do that, he's good with that shit, reading people anyways."

I sit down on the chair next to him and just stare straight. What have we gotten ourselves into?

Jax sees my expression, "go up to the room and relax for a little while, we got it covered for now. You'll need your strength later for the meeting tonight."

I don't even acknowledge him. I just stand up and head straight back to my room. This is not the outcome I was hoping for. This is the worst possible outcome that we could have ever had.

We have a lot of connections but none that even equal half of the power the Ivanov's have. I honestly don't know what we're going to do. I feel like this is my fault, the problem that I brought upon my family.

I know that's not true, but I can't help the way I think. I stay fully clothed as I crawl into my bed. Jax is right, I need to sleep. I need to get out of my head for a while.

CHAPTER 31

*a*nna

The conference room is starting to fill up as Jax holds his emergency meeting. Mason just arrived and all of us siblings are here.

We decided before not to tell my father about any of this, he doesn't even know that I was kidnapped for almost three weeks. He's really enjoying retirement. There's no need to worry him and there's nothing more that he can do that Jax can't.

The conference room table can hold sixteen people. Jax sits at the head of it. With Colt on his left and Mason on his right. I sit next with Colt while Finn sits next to me on the other side. My two brothers box me in.

Dima Ivanov and his sergeant in arms have arrived. I notice Dima and Mason keep glaring at each other.

This should be fun. The Italian and Irish have also arrived with their right-hand men. Everyone has taken a seat, we're just waiting on the Mexican Mafia and a few of the heads for the lower-class gangs. Jax didn't want to leave anybody out.

Everybody talks and jokes. They occasionally look around the room, not quite sure why they're here. Us Moretti's are totally quiet and just watching everyone. We have bad news and we need help from all of these people.

We've done countless jobs for everyone in this room. Most of it was kidnapping jobs where gangs are pitted against gangs. The Irish mafia kidnapped one of the women of the Italian mafia.

We were able to get her back and later learned that it was her choice. She'd fallen in love with one of the guards from the Irish mafia.

It's just the way this world works, that even after dealing with an almost war and massive bloodshed, they can sit in the same room together and be friends or at least at the very minimal, acquaintances.

I can hear the door open as several men I've never seen come in. These must be the lower-class gangs that Jax was telling me about. Colt also mentioned to me never to underestimate them. They might not have the resources that the rest of us do, but they could still pack a good punch.

I can hear a familiar voice talking behind me as the

door opens. It must be the Mexican Mafia. Then, that same annoying laughter comes through, Cruz.

Cruz and his guy take a seat down at the other side of the table. He notices me and his face lights up, he smiles and gives me a wink.

I instantly fly out of my chair and pound my fist on the table. "You son of a bitch, you knew where I was the whole time and you didn't tell my brothers."

Cruz just laughs. I don't think that fucker knows any other type of response except laughing. "It's all about the money baby." He tells me like I should understand.

Colt and Finn both grab one of my hands, pulling me back down into the seat as Colt whispers in my ear. "The past is the past, there's nothing we can do about it. You know how these things work."

I say I do but it still pisses me off. I just want to take one shot at that bastard, just one. I'd punch him right in the throat or maybe I could just rip off a testicle, I've never done that before.

Jax doesn't look too happy with Cruz or my outburst. I had a feeling he knew who came to Maxim's house. There's not that much he could do about it, *yet*. I know we'll find a way to get even with that bastard.

After everybody has taken their seats, a few of them are still standing around, there's not enough room for everyone, Jax stands up.

He looks over at Dima, "I would like to know what the hell is going on with your brother and why he kidnapped my sister?" Jax yells before slamming down his fist on the table, totally making it look like I lightly smacked the table earlier.

The room is dead silent, as everybody watches Jax with mild curiosity and uncertainty. We might not be Mafia, but we are powerful enough to have eliminated threats before. Like most people in here, to save our family, we won't even think twice about it.

"To be honest, man, I don't know," Dima says somberly.

Jax slowly sits back down in his seat but leans forward and places his elbows on the table. "According to Anna, your brother wants all of us dead. Apparently, he blames us for Sophia."

This causes a few gasps from those in attendance. Dima shakes his head, he's lost for words.

"Why in the fuck did you guys hire us?" Jax is fuming, his face is a light shade of red. If he gets any madder, I'm afraid he's going to have a heart attack. I watch him for a few minutes and imagine he's in a cartoon. His head actually blows from the anger. I chuckle under my breath, not letting anybody hear.

"I hired you guys because we needed somebody who knew what they were doing, and Maxim was out of the country." Dima gets up walks behind his chair, gripping it hard enough where his knuckles turn white. I could tell he's pissed, too.

"He's someone you don't want to mess with." This is

different, I can actually see the fear in his eyes. Even some of Maxim's family is afraid of him?

Dima continues, "I know after talking to you that there's somebody on the inside. You guys have a mole, or we have a mole. According to our family legacy, we hold everybody involved responsible."

Jax nods, "that means if your brother wants to kill us, he's also going to have to kill you."

"Correct," Dima states as he slumps back down in his chair. The room is still silent, as all of the men look between the acting head of the Russian mafia and the head of the Moretti family.

Colt and Finn still have a hold of my hands, they never let go. It's a little bit more reassuring. I'm also glad I'm not the only female in here. The Irish boss' right-hand man or I should say woman, is named Cassandra.

She is everything you would expect for someone being Irish, the red hair, a few freckles dabbed on her face and the crystal blue eyes.

She's built a lot more than I am and from what I hear, even deadlier. She would kick a puppy if it meant saving her boss. I fight hard to hold back another laugh, I could see her missing and falling on her ass. I really need to stop thinking to myself.

I look over at Jax as he starts to speak, "I want you to tell that fucking brother of yours that I'm not going to give him my sister. No matter what he threatens me with or what he offers. It's. Never.

Going. To. Fucking. Happen." Jax emphasizes the last part.

What? What is he talking about, giving me to Maxim? Colt slightly squeezes my hand and then whispers in my ear, "Maxim sent Jax a text message earlier, that if he were to give you back to him, the rest of us would be spared."

"Wow, I never saw that coming," I say in a whisper. If I did go back to him, then I wouldn't have to worry about the lives of my brothers. I can't get that damn thought out of my head.

"Don't even think about it," Finn whispers in my ear.

Jax looks over to the Mexican boss. "Cruz, I want to know for sure that you're on our side. You fucking owe us."

Cruz's deadly face is back, he no longer wears his sweet smile. "Yes," I know he has no choice if he ever needs help from us again.

Jax goes through each of the heads of the different families, except for Dima. They all agree to back us, even the smaller gangs.

I can see the relief on his face. He needed all their backing, but he also needed them to do it in front of Dima so that it will get back to Maxim.

Cruz stands up, looks over at Jax still in business mode. "It will definitely help with all of us backing you, but for God's sakes, the man has the freaking president on speed dial."

Jax, along with everyone in the room including myself wait for a Cruz to continue. "Eventually he will catch up with you guys. If he wants Anna bad enough, he will take her."

Jax listens and probably has come to the same conclusion that I and my other siblings have. That Cruz is right, one day he will catch up with us.

"Trying not to sound harsh man, but you might actually want to consider his offer." Cruz tries to plead.

"No, if it was your sister, would you do it?" I could tell that Jax has the urge to stand up and start pacing the room.

"Point made," Cruz grunts as he sits back in his chair. He wouldn't sacrifice one of his own sisters, so really how could he asked us to do that.

The meeting starts to taper down. The men spend the next hour talking about other issues between the families and out on the streets. It bores me to tears. I've never been one for meeting stuff, especially illegal meeting stuff.

I think everyone in the room would find it extremely rude if I got up and left since this whole meeting was called based on me.

All of those in attendance decided just to take up the regular monthly meeting that would happen in a few days from now and do it today so that they don't have to come back out.

Colt hates waiting just like I do, so we both grab our phones and start playing different games together.

We spent half of our time on hangman and the other half on tic tac toe. Just like when we were kids.

My phone buzzes causing me to get out of my game and check the message.

The cold sweat comes over me and chills run up and down my arms as I whisper, "oh no."

CHAPTER 32

*M*axim

I smile as I watched the whole emergency meeting that Jax arranged take place.

No one knows I'm able to see, them not even my brother. Everybody has a price, I just had to find the right one for one of the higher-ups right-hand man.

I know my brother wouldn't be talking shit if he knew I was watching. His ass would have just sat in that chair and been seen not heard.

He and I are going to have words later. He shouldn't be giving the Moretti's any information on us, whatsoever.

I seriously doubt if the other bosses knew I was watching they would agree to help Jax. That part doesn't really upset me, I can understand where they're coming from.

I know that if they don't help, they can no longer

continue using the services the Moretti's offer, and that would hinder a lot for these guys. Even though most of the stuff that Jax does is legal and good. There are a few times that he's helped several families find stolen and lost shipments.

I can't take my eyes off Anna. I told my guy to make sure he sat on the opposite side of her. We gave him a small camera that's mounted inside of a tie clip. The view is pretty good, straight in front of him, whenever he turns, I can't see her anymore.

I know I said he's got to look natural, especially when someone starts speaking, but I want eyes on Anna all the time.

She looks gorgeous as usual. A little tired and out of place, maybe bored. I wonder how she feels actually finding out who I am? I knew I should have told her, I wish that I was the one that did.

My informant lets me know that she's scared, more for her brother's than herself.

I made sure to have audio included. I had to pay out the ass for this. It increases his chances of getting caught, especially in a high-profile meeting. They wouldn't even have a second thought, that guy would have been killed on the spot.

After listening to Jax and Dima go back and forth for a while, my attention is turned on Cruz. Even when she's not looking, he's constantly staring at her. This is irritating me more than anything as I watch the video play out on my laptop behind my desk.

Booker comes in and watches some of the tape with me. "Cruz needs to be taken care of," I tell him.

I'm not looking at him, but I can almost feel and hear his head nod. He hates the bastard just as much as I do. That man won't be on this Earth that much longer.

"Cruz has a part in this. Whether he likes it or not, he signed up and has some kind of connection to the stalker." I turn around in my chair and look at Booker before I continue. "He's the key to solving this."

Booker's face gets lighter, which shocks me. When he gets embarrassed, his dark skin turns a very light shade of pink, and when he's happy, his dark color lightens.

"I'll have men get on it right away. It's going to be harder to get this guy than others, but we'll figure it out." He says never taking his eyes off the video.

I turn back and face the computer. I know he'll figure it out, he's the best right-hand guy anybody could ever ask for. I'm willing to bet my life that nobody will be able to put a camera on him when we're in a meeting.

They tried that before. Booker always lets me know when somebody tries to infiltrate our meetings or find out information that's not for them. Then he handles it. It depends on how much they wanted is what kind of punishment they're going to get.

The camera focus is back on Anna, it looks like she

and one of her brothers are playing a game on their phones. Yep, I guessed it, she's bored off her ass.

I watch her in total fascination. The way she bites her lip when she's doing good or the way her brow creases when she's doing really bad.

I don't really pay attention to the video audio. They're just talking about useless stuff between the families and out on the streets.

I do listen to the conversation that Booker has with another one of our higher up guards.

"I want you guys to get Cruz," Booker pauses as he listens to the reply. "Yes, you heard me right. He actually screwed the boss and he's got some information that we need, really need." Deep inside I hope they get him before the Moretti's extract the information on who hired him.

Booker goes back and forth on schematics of the job and how to properly move forward. My focus gets off him and goes back to Anna. I've never seen her look anything except downright gorgeous, even when she's mad, sick or even bored.

My dick painfully hardens against the zipper of my jeans. I have a feeling the fuckers going to burst if I don't get her back soon. No other woman will do it for me right now after I got a taste of her.

Anna is still on her phone, this is a perfect time for me to make my intentions known. Why wait any longer, she already knows that I'm coming for her.

I watched her as she sat in shock when Jax

explained the deal I try to make with him. I had a feeling he wouldn't go for it, but it was worth a try. There's no way in hell I would sell my sister's for my own safety.

I quickly type out a message and send it to Anna. I just hope that fucker remains sitting straight so I can watch her expression when she gets it.

I'm watching you. Did you miss me, baby? Soon, we'll be together again. -M

It takes a minute for Anna to open up the message. I laugh, it looks like she was finishing her game with Colt first.

As soon as she reads it, her head snaps up. She doesn't pay any attention to the guy right in front of her. Her gaze quickly travels to every set of eyes in the room, even the other girl.

Anna looks at everybody except for her brothers, then her gaze lands on Cruz, that's when the hatred shines through.

This is the only time that I'm irritated with the video. I wish I would have had more cameras installed. I can't see the expressions on anybody else's face except for the few sitting right next to her that are in view.

Anna's fist is clenching her phone hard. Her brother, Finn, notices it and makes her relax her grip. He takes the phone out of her hand, looking over the message I just sent.

He says something under his breath and then passes

it behind Anna over to Colt. Who then reads the message, too.

I can see where this is going, so I send off a quick message to my guy to be nonchalant. They might be on to him or at least they're on to somebody in the room. In all honesty, I don't give a shit if he's caught or not, I just want to watch Anna.

I can only make out some of Jax when he leans forward. He leans forward to read the message on the phone that Colt put on the table.

Booker finished his conversation and is watching with me. We both wait, shits about to hit the fan. All I can do is just watch my girl and hope that she's feeling the same way I am.

She doesn't look scared, which entices me more. We both share a deep connection. I can feel it in my bones that she wants me as much as I want her.

Soon, baby, soon.

NOTE FROM THE AUTHOR...

Anna's and Maxim's story continues in
Book 4: Entangled by Him
Thank you so much for reading!!!

Find out when the next books will be released. You will also learn about upcoming contests and a sneak peek into K.J.'s life. Click below.

Facebook | Amazon | Newsletter | Reader Group

ALSO BY K.J. THOMAS

Blackwood Academy

Hiding From Monsters

Running From Monsters

Taming the Monster

Moretti Siblings

Twisted Obsession

Cruel Obsession

Stoneridge Academy

Hate Me

Fear Me

Break Me

Release Me

ACKNOWLEDGMENTS

I want to sincerely let my Husband, and kids know how much I appreciate them, not for what they've done during my writing of these books, but what they've endured. I was 100% book focused and nothing else. I love you guys!